# Breeding Devotion

## Arian Mabe

This is a collection of short stories focusing on impregnation, breeding and sex while pregnant. Bipedal and some quadrupedal anthropomorphic characters feature in this collection.

This story collection covers straight sex, oral sex, vaginal sex, impregnation, breeding, pregnancy, first time sex, multiple partners, group sex, exhibitionism, oviposition, and love/romance.

**Table of Contents**

# The Stag and the Doe

Amelia moaned softly as her lover caressed her stomach, the stag anthro's antlers rising spectacularly above his head, the tines strong and bold. A red deer, he was powerful and solid, his hide bulging with muscle, though Amelia was smaller and lighter, a fallow deer that did not bear any antlers. Spots marked her rump, but they could not be seen as she stretched out across the bed, the sheets rumpling beneath her, twisting up in such a way that she could not be comfortable. Yet she did not have it in her heart to ask him to help her readjust, not with the comfortable touch of him nuzzling her pregnant stomach seducing her, softening the tenderness between them even more.

"David…"

She tried to work her tongue around his name, but the red deer was too powerful, moving over her, his tongue curling into her snatch as she tried to rock her hips up for him. Her head swam with raw passion, yet the love between them was not something that could be held back, not even at such a time. The rise of her belly trembled, heralding the spring of new life to come, and already she wondered whether the fawn she would birth would be a male or a female, the surprise something that they still wanted to hold close to their hearts.

At least for a little while longer. Just a little while…

"David… Ah… Please…"

Amelia whimpered, begging, her paws reaching for him, curling around the base of his antlers, though her trembling touch did not dare hold him there. The tingles of submission vibrating so very sweetly and softly through her were too alluring, a bigger and bigger part of her wanting to submit, to drop down before him, to worship the stag who had put his seed in her womb and brought forth new life. Of course, it was her that was carrying it, but having him as her protector would always make her weak at the knees.

Some things… Well, they just worked.

He was soft and sweet, deliberately sensual as he lapped deeply up into her pussy, one paw spread protectively over her stomach even as he pleased her, brought her to a squirming tease of delight. The doe's thighs closed on either side of his head, soft and plush, her body naturally curvy but even more so with the fullness of her breasts in the later stages of her pregnancy showing through. They hung down heavily, round and full, even her nipples begging attention from the soft swirl of his tongue. Yet David could not do everything at once, muscles bulging obviously through even his coat of fur, the thicker ruff around his neck proudly dominant − but not in a way that he had to scream and shout about it.

No… Anyone that saw him knew that he was the one in charge and with that sense of power and control came responsibility too. The responsibility to love and care for his sweet, sweet doe until the end of his days, to dote on her, to please her, to give her everything that she could have ever wanted in the world and more. He wanted her and he'd taken her, swept her up in his arms and shown her something that she'd never had before, but that was just how everyone was when they were in love. They left the rest of the world, their old lives, behind, bringing everything together into a new sense of being, everything different with their one, true love.

At least, that was how it was for David and Amelia, for the stag himself could not remember at all what life had been like before he'd got together with Amelia. His tongue slurped up deeply into her even as he recalled the very first time he'd laid eyes on her, a sports-buck, a jock through and through. Of course, she hadn't given him the time of day, not back then in college, and she cried out as he lapped sweetly around her clit.

He knew her better than he did back then. *Much* better, in fact.

Amelia panted heavily, her moist nostrils fluttering with little pulses of breath. His tongue did such wonderful things to her that she was hardly present in her reality, the soft, purple bedsheets crumpled under her body. Her hips tried to rise, but the weight of her belly, the little one inside, weighed her down, even though her heart still sang so dreamily of the promise of new life. It would come, of course, in time and there was no rushing them out, not when the delight of it all was so stringent in its presentation.

"Ah…" She wanted to say more but she could not, fingers brushing the stag's head as his tongue swirled around her clit, plunging back deep inside. "Ah… Please… More… David…"

He knew what she needed, despite her lack of any ability to convey that to him, warm breath tickling her damp folds, juices flowing freely. Grunting into her sex, his soft, wide nose tickled her clit with a tease of sensation while he lapped deep up inside her, his tongue very nearly reaching to her innermost barrier, though he could not quite stretch it that far. His shaft throbbed up against his own stomach, trapped between him and the bed, but David's mind was not on that, panting hotly into her sex.

No… All that mattered, right then and there, was his heavily pregnant doe, the sweetheart who lit up his life. He could have been lost to lust and yet he zeroed in on her with devotion in his gaze, seeing only her. The strong softness of her thighs drew him in more and more, her scent overwhelming him, though not even David could deny himself the tiniest of smirks as he pleasured her, the little cries and twitches that she gave telling him more than her words. He had learned long ago that she was not the most communicative when…well…

And who could blame her? Amelia grunted and groaned, making deeper, more guttural, sounds than before. She wanted to be pretty and delicate and feminine, but it simply was outside the realm of any possibility for her to hold back, whimpering and whining, panting, rocking her hips, craving every last bit of what her lover had to give her. The thickness of his length was surely waiting for her, girthier than those of other stags she had been with, back in college, before she'd gotten with him…but that didn't matter. They fit together perfectly and her mind could not wrap itself around anything else, not even when the opportunity to do so was offered up to her.

He had her right where he wanted her, their pleasure intertwined in such a way that there was no telling where one body ended and the other began, lovers at their best. David grunted and snorted against her body, excited in the rise of his hot breath, muscles bunching and tensing, pushing against her. He rolled his hips as if he was imagining, even then, just how it would feel to push inside her, but that was not the matter of the moment and why he had his tongue driven up into her sex, slurping and moaning.

No… Oh no. He had far more in mind than that, lashing her clit with adoring attention, his sweet doe panting breathlessly. Yet she would be even more breathless at the peak of orgasm, hips juddering, her tail twitching under her buttocks, trapped against the bedsheets. Not even she would want to hold back for pleasure, however, and it was with a feminine squeal that was a little too high-pitched for his sensitive ears that she climaxed. Somehow, Amelia's cloven hooves managed to dig down into the bed, offering her some support and stability to buck and grind up into his muzzle, her juices flowing, soaking his fur.

Not that David minded that in the slightest, of course, grunting against her, a stag in rut, cock hard and wanton. His fertile doe was so very ready to be bred again, even if he could not truly seed her again until their fawn was born, but that did not stop him from being too excited by her, pheromones thick in the air. He might have thought how funny it was what hormones could do if he was not wrapped up in more intoxicating things, but David was more caught up in slurping up every last drop of her honey that he could.

Her chest juddered in pant after path, but her stag was there to hold her firm, to steady her through the storm of orgasm. There was no losing her, not when David was there, and Amelia whimpered, pulsing wave after wave of orgasm trembling through, taking over her body. At times, it was quite as if she didn't know what to do with the ecstasy at all, muscles tense, contractions pulling taut where she was not even thinking about them, a part of her body and mind wanting to pull away too. It was just that strong that her body wanted to pull from what was making her feel that way – but that was where a partner came into play, helping her ride out the storm and the choppy waves of burning pleasure.

When she collapsed on the bed, however, the warm wash of the afterglow lapping over her, David was there all over again, licking her sweetness off his lips. His arms slid around her as he drew her in against his chest, her back to him, spooning her lightly. He was a good foot and a half taller than the curvy doe and still strong, the casual eye able to see his muscle even through the winter garb of his thick coat, but he held her delicately, savouring her presence against him. Sometimes, that feeling alone was all that was needed.

Still, his paw traced the outline of her belly, nuzzling the back of Amelia's neck where the spill of her brunette locks tumbled down, a little curly, not as well-groomed as the proper doe would have liked. But that was all well and good for the two of them, the boundaries of being perfectly put together crumbling as their relationship developed. There was only so much, after all, that one could do when they lived together, learning to laugh and love together more comfortably.

The heat remained between them, however, as it always did. Maybe that heat was what had resulted in the rising swell of her pregnant belly or maybe it had simply been meant to be: they did not care to dig into it. All was as it needed to be as he grunted and ground his shaft lightly into her plump buttocks, relishing in the softness of them, needing his doe even more.

Amelia yielded to him, even though he had not even asked. He could have taken what he wanted, of course, but that was not in the nature of their relationship, their mutual pleasure encased in a give and a take of domination and submission. It didn't matter to them whether anyone else understood it or not as that was what worked for them, Amelia whimpering, eyes half-closed, drawing her upper leg, as she lay on her side, up closer to her belly, offering herself to him.

"Take me…"

The tip of his thick prick hungrily sought out her pussy, questing for entry, though they had fucked and made love so many times during their relationship that their bodies knew one another as intimately as their minds. His shaft pushed into her as she cried out his name and, once again, their bodies were one, the taste of her essence marking his muzzle.

She had marked him and he her, each in their own way.

David, however, was still a stag in rut, a feral need to cum rolling through him as he thrust, pushing deep into her pussy, her folds closing around him. Her sex still twitched ever so faintly in the aftermath of orgasm, muscular contractions that no body could ever claim to be completely in control of, yet he felt it. He shuddered. Oh, he felt it *intimately*…and, as always, there was no going back the moment his shaft sank into her.

Amelia tried to hold firm, but she could not help a rampant bleat from breaking her lips as he pushed deep, filling her, the succulent length of his rod finding every sensitive spot that she didn't know existed. Why did his cock do so much for her when her fingers had never been adequate? Some would have said that that was merely because she didn't know her body well enough but maybe there was something more there, the connection between two furs, a stag and a doe who loved each other, that she had been missing all along.

As his shaft powered into her, a dominant paw cradling her belly, Amelia knew that it did not matter. Nothing else mattered but her stag, bleats breaking her lips as she cried out her lust and love for him. David's shaft powered deep, claiming her again and again even as she gave herself up to him, wanting nothing more than everything he had already given her. And yet David found something regardless to keep things fresh and new, the power of his thrusts thrumming through her with every stroke.

"Oh… Yes, David, yes!"

"Unff… Amelia, you're still so…tight!"

Maybe modern life had had them believing the media too much but, of course, she did not soften or loosen, not beyond anything required for their comfort, during her pregnancy and their time making love. Her sex closed tightly around him, squeezing down, though she was deliberate that time, the aftershocks of orgasm still pulsing through her lightly. The lure was there, however, pulling at her, driving her to want to climax again, if only to get yet another hit of that high, which was never elusive to her. Not when David was with her, of course, for he broke down all barriers that may have been in their path.

He couldn't thrust as hard as he may have liked in such a position, and yet it was one of the most intimate positions, David not even caring as his lover lay on his arm, trapping it under her body, though his fingers squeezed each breast in turn. He couldn't help himself and neither did he have to, whispering and groaning out her name repeatedly, lusting and loving her more and more. There was no stopping the passion between them, not as the slick slide of his cock powered on, into her sex. He filled her perfectly as her folds seemed to suck at him, a tight seal around his shaft. Yet he felt every inch of his length as he sank into her, a hoof kicked back, trying to dig into the bed for leverage, though it was not quite his to take.

Soon. But not quite then. That moment was for long, deep strokes, letting his cock power smoothly into her, to feel every last bit of her, inside and out. Adoringly, David's paw stroked down over the round of her stomach, feeling the presence of the life they had created within, wanting more. Maybe they would have another fawn after the first or maybe the first would fill them up so much that they would never want for anything ever again, though the breeding craving would still be there for his fertile, sweet doe.

She was delightful, so warm, so tight, her juices slick around him. The wetness of her cunny trickled down around the base of his cock, sheath pulling back ever so lightly as David used every inch of his cock that he was able to. Not an inch was to go to waste even as pleasure rose and rose inside him, wanting to push on to delight as much as he wanted to hold back.

But it was not to be contained as he, reluctantly, slipped his paw down between her legs, leaving the swell of her stomach be for the moment, though there was no doubt in his mind that his paw would return there. He had to adore it, protect her, every last bit that stretched out between them. Her pleasure too was there to flourish, however, even as he thrust and thrust, driving deep, stretching her out, fingers playing across her clit, desperate too, in a way, to see her scream in her high.

One orgasm, after all, would never be enough, not when it was so devoutly passionate, his doe shuddering against him. The tremor of her breath was too much for him, tail flicking up, every little shift in her body, the pull of her weight, something that he caught.

"Ohhhhhh!"

She couldn't stop it from coming, amazed even then that he was able to get her off for a second time so swiftly – and she couldn't even put that down to pregnancy hormones! She whimpered and moaned, lips parted, ecstasy pounding her, driving through out of rhythm with his cock, though the pulse and pound of that demanded its own kind of attention. But David was not about to stop as he tugged her back onto him, arm across her thigh while his fingers played her clit like an instrument, every thrust driving deep.

He could not stop, not even as his doe climaxed, passion rising, the light aroma of sweat colouring the air. It was intoxicating even then, teasing at the delight of it all, her sex seeming to tighten around him as the moment slipped beyond Amelia's control. David sucked in a breath but there was no holding in the divine bellow that tore itself from his throat, the ruff around his neck trembling, need powering through.

Ropes of virile cum, that were not needed but lusted for, all the same, flowed forth, spurt after spurt, splattering into her cunny, the tight velvet of her pussy. Against him, his doe shuddered, rolling her hips back, though she was just as trapped as she had been with his muzzle between her legs, her stomach bearing her down. Yet it was something that brought a heightened sense of pleasure to it, sweeping ecstasy pouring through, filling up their shared cup, the wine of lust overflowing in luscious swathes.

Amelia moaned, her eyes half-closed, needing it all, grunting, more feral and carnal than she usually was, but her lover was there too for her, holding her fast, steadying her through it. She felt it in the strongness of his chest against her back, how he pushed into her shoulders, a paw on her breast, nipples perky even as her body *burned*. They tingled up against his paw as she panted heavily, though there was no part of Amelia that would have changed anything about the position, the situation, the seething lust of it all.

The evidence of his virility lay in her stomach, however, her womb swollen with their shared love. His seed served no purpose pouring into her at that point, but they shared and delighted in it all the same. It was there for them, their bonding, their passion, his shaft driving in harder and faster even as David relished in the sweetly blissful release of that ultimate high. Cum trickled down the length of his shaft, marking the folds of her sex, even glistening on her clit, though it was the neck of his sheath that soaked with them. It was a strange sensation to have even a small amount of his own seed trickle back into his sheath and the stag shuddered, eyes closed, lips parted in a throaty bellow that signalled, at least for the time being, the end of the rut.

Yet his orgasm did not die down slowly and patiently but thrummed forth with the true breeding power of a stag, the tines of his antlers quivering. David could no more deny it than he could withdraw his love for Amelia, clutching his doe all the more tightly to him, fiercely protective. The warmth of her body moulding perfectly to his was something he wanted to keep for his own for the rest of his life, breath wafting over her neck, her shoulder, lips pressing to the nape of it in a tender kiss.

"Ohhh… Oh… Dave…David…"

She wanted to say something, anything, something to convey the depths of her love to him, but her words were lost in a moan. Such a rush of pleasure stole everything from her only to give it all back again in her next breath, her next heartbeat, all as it was supposed to be. How could anything at all be any different then perfectly right, after all, with the stag that she had given her heart and her life to?

It was right, all right. She moaned, leaning back into him, tipping her nose up, licking her lips, high softening, bringing her down and down and down.

Back into his arms.

She drifted from reality, barely breathing even as her chest heaved, whimpering softly, though she didn't need to worry about anything. David was there to hold her, to keep her and their little one safe, the big, brave stag that she had fallen head over hooves for crooning to her. A warbling kind of groan, like that of wild deer, not of anthro-kind, rose from his lips, though one could have called it a kind of purr too.

What it was proved to be of no consequence, only the peace between them, his softening shaft drooling within her, passion easing, though there was still a high there to be had in their love. Her eyelids fluttered closed, sleep calling, yet it was a slow, long glide down, not one that had any haste or rush behind it. It was only for the two of them, whimpering and moaning together, conveying their passion for each other in the most carnal, devout of ways, his paw finally returning to her belly. For there was a precious little one in there to bring them closer together in a new kind of way, even if they had already thought that there was nothing at all that could ever change the nature of their relationship to make it better than it already was.

Things changed, all the time… That could not be helped. Yet what was to come would see them in a new era of being, another kind of relationship, what they had both dreamed of for so many years.

Inside her, his shaft softened, slipping out, yet the warmth of their bodies was still to be shared, closer than ever, her buttocks grinding back against him even as she slumbered. Sleep, like so much else, could not be held off in the aftermath of all else, David nuzzling the back of her neck tenderly. He conveyed all he needed to her without words but letting his darling, sweet doe sleep was more important than speaking up right then and there.

He chuckled, sleep taking him too, dragging him softly down and down and down, a pleasant ache thrumming through his body. It was alright. There would be plenty of time to talk in the morning, the hour already late. Carefully, without jostling Amelia, the stag turned off the side lights, what had given the bedroom a softly illuminating glow for their romantic lovemaking. He would, however, have to trust that the heat of his body was enough to keep her warm, for he could not bear to wake her when she had already drifted off so lightly.

He'd care for her, look after her, his arms gently folded around her in the dark of the night. Nothing and no one would ever bring any harm to his Amelia.

David's paw rested on her stomach, feeling their little one squirm within. He smiled.

He'd always protect her and their fawn.

# Dragon Lovers

Lauren purred, the dragoness sitting back in the water of the corner bath, the whirlpool jets, at least for the moment, turned off. The water could froth and bubble when she had them on, though it was advised, for a dragoness in her condition, that she did not partake in hot tubs, which the bath was close enough to when switched into that mode. So, all the green dragoness had to do was to allow the water to lap over her scales, gently caressing the rise of her pregnant belly, showing her a little more of herself, her body, all that had to come to pass as her hands held her stomach lightly.

Her muzzle was long and elegant, her horns delicately curved and so small that sometimes they could not be seen in her thick, curly, sapphire hair that spilt down her neck, but her lover's lips matched hers perfect. Morgan might have been a non-anthro dragon, unlike her as a typical anthro with small wings that she could not fly with, but he was her perfect match, there was no doubt about that. With deep, rich brown scales in shades of copper and bronze, he appeared as if he might have appeared from a dragon's hoard itself. It was because of him, built like a typical feral dragon but with wings that could take them airborne, that their house had to be adapted.

He fit most places though, the size of a large horse – which was manageable when it came to their household, at least! His horns were thicker and chunkier than hers, though that was no matter at all, his jaw strong and masculine while his wings were usually folded in against his back. Yet the drake had such a wingspan on him that he could take them both up into the sky together, whether his loving wife rode on his back or clung to his claws, relishing in the drama of flight.

But that was not the moment as she leaned back against him, the bathroom doorway wide with a double door to accommodate him, a wet room with a large shower that he could more easily clean off with. There was no bath that they could afford, unfortunately, that could accommodate both, though they had plans, one day, to have a house with a pool.

"One day, darling," Morgan breathed, a hint of fire on his breath, though there was no need for him to warm his lover at that time. "One day... One day, soon... We're going to meet her."

Lauren giggled, cupping his face as he pushed over her shoulder.

"Sweetie, you don't even know if they're a drake or a dragoness yet... We can't tell with the ultrasound, not yet!"

He chuckled, shaking his head, a glint dancing in his eye. The drake's tail curled back and forth, tipped with a spade-like end, brushing her cheek.

"No... No, sweetheart, but I can't wait to meet them."

And just like that, his lips touched hers and they forgot where they were in the moment, water streaming from her body as Lauren rose to meet him, passion coursing through her. Her hair was soaked and plastered to her back and shoulders where it had dipped into the water, though the rest of it further up was left dry. Her tail lifted from the water as if possessed by a higher power, curling around his, wanting to claim the larger drake, her lover and husband, as much as he wanted to claim her too.

They were claimed, but not yet claimed. Together and apart, the two of them always more than willing to come together in passion all over again. He groaned into her mouth as his body reacted to her, Lauren's heart pounding, a thick length of dragon meat pushing out from the slit at the base of his belly, close to the join of his hind legs but positioned a little further forward for the ease of mating bliss.

"Mmm… Stay there, love," Morgan breathed, breaking the kiss briefly, clambering up on the edge of the tub with one forepaw, eyes burning with lust and love for his wife. "Lift your hips for me."

It was not a command, but it most certainly was a suggestion she wanted to follow, trembling as her heavy body was at least a little supported by the water. Oh, he felt good to run her hands down his face, memorising the curves of his cheeks once more, how it gave him a stronger jawline, the thick ridges of scales over his eyes that took the place of eyebrows with anthro type dragons, giving them more expression. Yet her body was as naked as his, even though the thick beast of his shaft had her whimpering already, his nose questing down as she supported herself, back against the far side of the bath.

With her back to the wall, braced on the small lip and shelf, her scales gleamed wetly, her legs spread, his tongue darting between for the treat of her sex. Morgan wasted no time at all in showing his heavily pregnant wife how much he adored her, his tongue driving up into her sex with a lewd, wet slurp.

"Oh, god!"

Why was it so much better with Morgan than it had been with anyone before him? Not that she was thinking of past lovers, of course not, only in the way that it was impossible to ever say that anyone could be better than him. His tongue plundered her hot depths so sweetly, curling inside her, seeking out her G-spot as if he had already known that she was feeling on the friskier side that night.

Morgan always knew and she clutched at his horns for support, even though the tub was slippery.

His head helped pin her in place, ensuring she would not slip off and back down into the bath, the hard push of the drake's head driving her to gasp and press up against him. He didn't need to lap over her clit as his tongue flicked up wantonly inside her, desire coursing through with every pump and thrust of her hips. He pressed into her clit with his nose and lip while his tongue went to work, sending her head spinning.

"Oh, yes… God, yes… Morgan…"

The drake peered up at her, though he would not stop, needing it all, grunting against her, his tail swaying to his back, though he was in a perfectly comfortable position with his head stretched out towards her. Water lapped under his neck, though the drake would not stop, bringing her closer and closer, lapping eagerly as he purred, letting those vibrations travel into her sex, up to her G-spot. He could mostly only feel that part of her when she reacted to him touching the right spot, the right pressure, the right vibration… It was all about knowing his lover, his partner, the one that he wanted to spend every day of the rest of his life with.

Nothing else would do for them, water splashing and lapping over the edge of the tub. Her hips rose, braced against his head, tongue curling inside her as her toes did the same.

"Yes… Morgan… Hon… Honey!"

She cried out, her head tipping back, though she was careful of the cool tiles of the bathroom wall, not wanting to cause an accident at that time. Orgasm ripple through her, the pounding pulses coming in waves, her legs trembling, losing control of even the tiniest of muscles in her body at a point where she really wanted to be in control. But that was the beauty of orgasm in how it forced her to give everything up, to be her bare and true self at all times. She could whimper and she could grunt and she could make all manner of sounds that she could not usually make, letting go while she wrapped her legs around his head and neck. Pressing in close, she trusted him to hold her, lapping sweetly through her orgasm.

Yet she was not done when she softened from the high of climax, sultrily lowering her eyelashes, even though there was no smoke to curl from her nostrils.

"Darling…"

Morgan shivered. Oh, he knew what that meant, even as his wife slipped from the tub, his cock hard and throbbing, questing for her already. What his darling wife wanted, however, she got – always. That wasn't an option for him not to give her what she craved, tending to her every need. It was a good thing, surely, how well they fit together, as if every heartbeat and every breath were in perfect time with one another.

Slipping to the floor of the bathroom, not caring for the water, she drew him over her gently, on all fours with her pregnant belly rounding down under her. And it was there, under the flow of hot water as Morgan twitched on the shower dial with the flexible tip of his tail, that his cock finally pressed up against her sex, the perfect size for a dragoness like her to take.

It stretched her as he eased in, the warmth of his body shielding her from the heat of the shower, but she still cried out, her body desperate for it, despite her recent orgasm. She would always lust for her husband, the bulk of his body protecting her, cries echoing off the walls of the bathroom, which were all tiled. That helped with cleaning and yet the heat of condensation dripped down the walls as the running shower filled it with the sultry touch of steam, his hips pushing, thrusting, filling her with every stroke.

She moaned, yet his guttural groans were just as alluring, making her feel as if she was right where she needed to be, somewhere else separate from reality. He powered into her with strong strokes, though not too deep, knowing exactly how deep he could go without hurting her, careful of the egg within her womb at all times. For he had never wanted to pound her crudely, only take her tenderly, even if raw passion did flow to the surface at times.

Yet Lauren shivered so beautifully under him that he could not help but curl his tail under his body and around her, squeezing her tightly, letting her know, without words, that he loved her dearly. Even as their bodies joined, her sex slick, hot and tight around him, his sweet dragoness moaning out through another orgasm, thrust there already. His smooth shaft fit inside her perfectly, though it had taken her some time originally to learn how to take him.

The stretch, however, was different with reptiles like them, their bodies adjusting, always appeasing a partner, soothing and stretching comfortably. Larger members could fit seemingly smaller holes, though he did not dare go as deep as normal simply due to the weight in her belly.

That could come again, another time. They would need that, stroke after stroke, the powering high, what lifted them to the sky above, wings spread and roars trembling in their throats. Lauren whimpered breathlessly, her smaller wings twitching against his underbelly, though he curled around her lovingly as if he was trying to protect her from something in the world that she had not paid due mind to.

But it was their moment, their cries bouncing off the walls, everything coming together so very sweetly, empowering them. It was all they needed to be together, moaning, panting, breaths coming in heady snatches and gasps. He thrust harder and harder, losing track of himself in the heat of the moment, though he knew in his heart that Lauren would tell him if she needed him to go easier.

Yet it was at the moment that their joint orgasm hit in swamping waves of bliss, his shaft throbbing, sending his seed into her passage, that they knew they would not have wanted it any other way. Thrust after thrust had her grinding passionately back onto his length even as he bumped up against her innermost barrier, the push and almost hasty shove making her stomach jump, though she was never at any risk.

Ropes of hot cream flooded her pussy, further slickening the path of his cock, her pregnancy betraying her fertility and his virility, though the ship had sailed for her to fall pregnant. She would already lay an egg for her loving husband, the dragon of her dreams, eyelids fluttering as pleasure lay heavy upon her.

Their moment. Only theirs. No one would take it from them, not then, not ever, whimpering, whispering, shivering in the softening glow. It was there and they would savour it each and every time, her lust rising through her pregnancy, wanting her husband even more than usual.

Morgan could deal with that, nuzzling her head, squeezing his tail around her as if he was trying to drag her in even closer to him and his body, two bodies becoming one. He'd never want anyone other than his wife, the two of them becoming slowly aware again of the rush of hot water, the hiss of it, steam floating in swathes around them.

Their love would go on forever, dragon with dragoness, always together.

And they couldn't wait to make their family of two a three.

# Loving Breeding

The dragoness, Elsa, purred, stretching out in the sand of the beach, the waters of the lake lapping softly, serenely, at the shoreline. It was as tender as a lover's kiss as the water tickled over the sand and the pebbles, worn smoother and smoother by the passage of time, and she lazily rolled onto her back, exposing the lighter blue scales of her underbelly, grains of damp sand clinging to her scales. Her back was a darker shade of blue, something that helped camouflage her in the water when she was hunting fish and even larger mammalian prey, though that warm, sweet day she was fat and content, no longer needing to satisfy her stomach.

The land provided there and the tickle of heat in her belly had drawn Elsa to her mate, her horns softly curled and a line of spines running down her neck, her back and the length of her tail. Gionne purred as he leaned over her, the bulk of the red and purple dragon's scales splashed through with mixed colours as if he had been dipped in the natural paints of the living world. His horns were larger, heavy on either side of his head, and rounded like those of a ram, the light ridges on them drawing the eye down, enticing it to follow. At the tip of his tail was a club-like weapon, something that was more prevalent with male dragons than those who were female, though the gene for similar could be passed down to any sex of dragon.

"Hey there, beautiful," he purred, his warm breath tickling her cheek as she murmured and allowed Gionne to bear her back into the soft, damp sand. "Where have you been hiding?"

Elsa giggled, her tail sweeping back and forth in the sand, as if she was trying to make a particular shape down there. Yet her mate's eyes were hypnotic, her heart swelling passionately with both lust and love for him.

"Only waiting for you," she breathed. "I need it… Why don't you take just a little bit of that need away from me, darling?"

Gionne wouldn't do anything less than that, slipping down the length of her body with a passionate growl, his tail flicking back and forth, though he was a good third larger than her. He didn't feel like he dwarfed her, though their bodies fit together exactly as nature intended, the slit at the base of his belly, close to the junction of his tail, but there was a veritable size difference between them too that had to be considered. Thankfully, his long, draconian neck meant he could still press into her neck, crooning and kissing and nipping playfully, when he was inside her.

But, first, he had to get her ready, his nose questing lower, to the slit at the base of her own belly, tongue flickering out against the edge of it. Elsa did not need much teasing, not much readying, not as the edges of her slit parted so readily for him, aching for attention. The forked tip of his tongue eased inside, reverently lapping at her, though his words were spent in actions rather than said verbally, his love for her pouring through each and every lap of his tongue.

Elsa squirmed under Gionne's touch, her jaws parted, tongue flickering out. Panting softly, she ached into his touch, trying to curl her hind legs down enough to gain some purchase to thrust up against him, though that was not possible. Her legs simply didn't bend that way, leaving her more vulnerable on her back than she ever would have been in any other position. But Elsa didn't mind that, trusting Gionne with her heart, her body, even her soul. The drake would never do anything to hurt her, much less when the pleasurable, tingling laps of his tongue flicked up inside her, coaxing pulse after pulse of ecstasy from her.

She moaned, whispering her love to him, warm breath tickling the inside of her maw as she breathed through her mouth, need coursing through her. More than any other time, the need to breed ached through her, the stirring of nesting in the pit of her belly. Oh, her mate had to know it too, the scent of her pheromones laden on her juices, filling the air. Her need pounded the depths of her body, panting, heaving, flanks shuddering with every breath she managed to snatch into her lungs, though the only way Elsa could release excess heat from her body was through her jaws.

Still, it curled inside her, his tongue flickering tenderly up against that sensitive patch of nerves held within her pussy. They'd been together for so long, breeding and loving one another, that he knew her body intimately and Elsa still quivered like a virgin when he hit just the right spot inside her. Her heart lurched and she tangled her tail around his leg, dragging him to her, holding him against her body in the only way she could.

"Yes… Gionne… Yes!"

She had to have it, losing herself in the moment, the sun's warm rays caressing her scales. She was so close to the shoreline that they would very easily be able to roll straight into the water to cavort and cool off when they had had their pleasure from one another, but that was something for later. In the moment, all Elsa ached for was the throbbing spire of his cock, the tangle of orgasm, needing everything, one notion and emotion after another clouding her perception.

"Ah… Yes… Deeper…"

Gionne smirked playfully against her pussy as he pressed in closer, tail flicking gently behind him, though his cock ached desperately. The long, hard spire of cock meat was as needy as ever, yet he could not allow such a moment to pass without first pleasing his mate, slurping into her as her juices flowed more and more slickly, even more readily. Oh, she was ready for him, but Gionne crushed his nose softly against her scales for a moment first, lapping so deeply and swirling his tongue around and around that his mate surely would see stars.

He knew her intimately and she climaxed instantly, rolling her hips, trying to push up and grind onto his tongue. Damn! Stars burst behind her lowered eyelids, tongue dangling out of her mouth, so much so that she couldn't be careful about it, where her sharp teeth were. It was all she needed, heaving, whimpering, whining, letting pulse after pulse of delicious pleasure washing over her. It blistered through, snarling wildly, taking her for a flight that not even her wings could carry to her.

It was all she needed, all she craved, languishing in the burning, simmering afterglow, wings spread, trembling, out on the sand to either side of her body as she lay there. Dimly, Elsa was aware of her mate pulling back and she whined and scrabbled to get into the position she wanted to be in for him, on her stomach, sand all scuffed up around her, the shape of their bodies implanted into the ground until the rains came to wash it away.

Yet it would never wash away their lust as he covered her from behind, her tail pushed out of the way for him and twined around as much of his barrel as she could reach, drawing him in close. Gionne hissed through his teeth, rolling his hips, the hard, throbbing length of his cock desperate for it, drooling thick drip after drip of pre-cum, splattering into the sand. He rolled his head from one side to the other, scales lifting a little where he tried to release a more heat from his body, though that would not be needed shortly when there was so much heat in him that it burned all the way through him.

He speared deeply into her, her slick folds welcoming him inside, panting, grunting, his nostrils flaring with every grabbed breath, though his lungs had more than enough. He heaved over her, needing every inch of her pussy, though she took everything readily, well-prepared and needy, her pussy massaging him even then. Gionne's eyes rolled back in his head, unable to hold back in the moment. There would never again be another dragoness in the whole wide world that could match up to how hot Elsa was with her pussy, the sexy blue dragoness controlling her muscles so intimately that she could massage his cock and get him off without him even moving an inch.

Gionne was too eager to sit there, however, rolling his hips, thrusting deep, claiming her with every trembling inch of his body, wings mantled over his back. His tail lashed and struck the air, the club slowing its swing, yet he was right where he wanted to be as he thrust and ground, following the rhythm of breeding that had been present with dragons for millennia already. Why change what was already perfect, after all?

Her sex closed around him, rippling and pulling as if she was trying to coax him deeper with every stroke. Elsa whimpered breathily and he lowered his head down to hers, pressing his cheek against hers, though it put a kink in his longer neck to do so. It was all worth it for his dragoness, his goddess, his queen, pushing into her, every thrust bringing their bodies closer together than ever. Breeding and mating were something special indeed and were not to be trifled with, eagerly anticipated, already, raising a clutch of little dragons, all chittering and squawking and hungry for their attention. It would not stop them from spending time with one another, of course, but it would bring them closer and closer, their relationship developing over the years.

The moment, however, as it was, was all about passion, raw and raunchy, sliding into her with every thrust, the heat of his lover intoxicating in the best of ways. Gionne hissed and grunted, giving a little shudder when her folds caressed him in such a way that it hit a particularly sweet spot, though his tail swinging back and forth betrayed his need. There was only so long a dragon like him could go on for, flanks heaving for breath, his lover meeting his eyes with a wicked glint in her own.

"Cum in me, darling," she breathed, body ripe and warm with breeding need. "Seed me *full*. I want to raise another clutch with you…"

So it was that, in the months to come, her body would rise with the swelling of pregnancy all over again, seeing her young grow, her eggs develop before they were laid. But all that mattered in a moment like that was the thrust of his cock, how he ground so deeply into his lover that Elsa was thrust over the edge into another orgasm, crying out, horns glinting in the sunlight. She would have dug them down back into the sand if she had been on her back, though he half-pinned her while she laid on her front, her pussy tight around him, muscles grabbing and massaging as if there was nothing else that her body could possibly do in a moment like that.

It was perfect, everything as it was meant to be, warmed by the sun as he heaved and tucked his head down, quivering on the brink. Yet not even Gionne could hold back from that high of delight, slamming in, letting her caress his entire length all the way to his peak. Finally, the drake let out a blast of a roar that echoed across the quiet waters of the lake, spending his need inside her, flooding her full as her body ached for it.

Streams of cum dripped from her pussy even as he spent himself inside her, thrusting and grinding slower and slower until he came to a halt. He grunted, shuddering as he stilled, tail lashing back and forth until it too came to a stop, the tight grip of his lover's pussy more than enough to get him to the point where he trembled and ached to let every last drop spill forth.

She milked him of his cum, drop after drop flowing deep, seeding her clutch, their clutch, their sweet eggs. They would grow, one day, into big, strong dragons, but that would be something for the future, when their bodies twisted and writhed together, undulating in bliss. She moaned, letting him lean against her, his body collapsing into her, moulding to the heat of her.

"I love you," she breathed, her mate rumbling his agreement. "So much."

Forever would drake and dragoness find each other in their claws, entwined until the end of days, but their moments of loving breeding would be all they needed. Time after time again.

# Breeding Gangbang

The vixen squirmed, tied to the breeding bench with her heart racing. On her back, she licked her lips, the spotlight encasing her, caressing her fur with a red glow that was deeper and more sensual than even her russet hues. The tip of her tail had been dipped, figuratively, in white paint and the white-cream of her belly stretched all the way up to the underside of her narrow, elegant jaw.

Of course, there was little that was elegant about her as she panted there, the dark room around the spotlight not allowing her to see further, blinded by the lust of her position. She whimpered and squirmed, twisting first one way and then the other, but there was no escape to be hand, not when the latex cuffs were tight and even locked into place along her wrists and ankles, even her thighs too to make quite sure that there was no way for her to twist out of position.

Her name? Her head swam, drifting, fading. No… Not then. Not ever. In the breeding closet…she had no name. She didn't need a name, not when she was "the breeder", the randy slut who was only there to get her pussy ploughed full of cock again and again.

She shivered. What more could a vixen hope for? Her legs were spread, lashed down tightly, the bench set with the bottom parted in a downward pointing "V", the midsection straight under her back and the top allowing her hand to easily be bound over her head. Her breasts rose heavy and full, tugged apart by gravity so that she had no cleavage but the size of them was drawn attention to, nipples perking to pink points through the divinely pure white fur of her chest. As she took in breath after breath, shuddering in place, the only other sound to cut through the chamber was the creak of the door opening.

Stiffening, she listened intently. Paw-steps. Closer…and closer.

"Evening, my red-haired beauty."

She whimpered. The dog had come prepared, clad only in a leather harness that went down his torso and looped around his hips, the points of the leather crossing marked by high-quality O-rings, the placing of each and every one skilfully deliberate. His lower half was completely bare, his hard cock out and ready. He seemed to be a bloodhound of some kind with long, flat ears dropping on either side of his head, but his expression was youthful, eyes gleaming with a kind of feral glee that tried to set her hackles up.

She knew what she was there for, the hound pushing a finger into her cunt, only bringing it to his lips after collecting a more than adequate sample of her deliciousness, suckling it clean.

"Mmm… It's been a while since I had a fresh bitch to breed."

He grinned as he moved between her legs, briefly adjusting the height of the bench to put her cunt on a better level for him, but the dog did not even pause to introduce himself, not properly, before spearing into her. The vixen cried out, hips trying to rise, but she was too firmly lashed down; those who had led her there, helped her up onto the bondage bench, having done far too good a job to let her be released that easily. No, her sodden pussy was to be bred and bred again, the dog howling with his head thrown back as he slammed into her, the slurp of her cunt tugging and pulling at his cock filling the room.

"Yes, oh, yes…"

Her head rolled, twisting, trying to contain the pleasure. There was nothing like being fucked when she was in heat and, already, she could feel it heightening, the prickle of urgent fire that felt quite as if she was being burned up from the inside out. It clawed at her like a feral creature straining for release and she gasped, throat contracting, struggling for breath that should have been hers to take under any circumstance at all. Yet she was there, lusting and moaning, taking all that she was given even then as if she had any choice in the matter anymore to say no.

Well, she'd had the choice earlier… But that very choice in her breeding had been one that the fox had wanted taken away from her. Thus, she'd been given exactly what she'd asked for.

"Mmm, is this the bitch?"

She jumped, not having heard the second dog enter, but she didn't get a chance to get a good look at him as her head was laid back all the way, the malamute (at least, she thought he was a malamute) thrusting into her maw. Sucking his dick upside-down, all the vulpine could do was groan around him, her tongue pressed over the top side of his cock, lapping and swirling, instinctively doing what was needed for her breeding lust.

"Unff… Good mouth on her."

"Good cunt too."

She shuddered. Could they talk to her like that? Oh, but why did it make her so hot, so wet? Her pussy drooled so thickly and over-productively that she could barely believe that all of it was hers, his cock pounding her viciously. Something thick bumped into her pussy-lips and the hound grunted, a paw closing around his growing not so as not to sink it inside her, tying them together, just yet. There were more, after all, that would want to savour her body and partake in all of the pleasure that that part of her could bring forth.

He didn't tell her that he was about to cum, heralding that only with a grunt and the deeper spearing of his cock into her wanton, soaked folds. Ropes of cum flowed forth, spurt after spurt filling her, his cream drooling out along the length of his cock as her pussy clamped down on him. Her head spun, caught up in an orgasm of her own, yet she could not drag her focus from the cock in her mouth, sucking and lapping, grunting softly with her hanging tail wagging and wagging.

"Huh, such a bitch in heat, hm?"

Yes, yes, she was… Her vision hazed over even when she opened her eyes all the way, that cock sliding from her cunt. Yet she needed it, oh: she needed it so badly! How could she possibly want a cock that much? It made no sense, no sense at all, gasping and grunting, her chest heaving as the malamute filling her muzzle moved. The door opened, welcoming another dog in, but she knew nothing more than his smell and the feel of his dick as it ploughed straight into her mouth, warming up on her tongue, in her maw, while the malamute took her pussy.

"Mmmph, you were right, so fucking tight!"

He threw his head back in a howl, hot and ready, a thicker length than the first hound's slamming in over and over again. There was no need for any of them to be gentle with her, after all, not even as she hacked and gagged and gulped around that monstrously delicious length plundering her muzzle. As much as the vixen twisted her head back and forth, all it took as a bearing down of the other dog's hips to keep her there, her pussy wrapped around a cock so fat that it set her head spinning.

More, she had to have more, so much more! Breeding lust set her skin tingling with illicit heat and the reason for her bondage was pulled into the light as she yanked and wrenched at it, eyes trying to strain, as much as her position did not allow her to see much of what was happening to her. If she could have wrenched herself free, ripping to escape, she would only have attacked the dogs for their lustful breeding rods, wanting more, craving it all. Yet they were there to satisfy her, even if the breeding passion of a vulpine was so legendary that to restrain her was merely the sensible course of action at such a time.

"Unff... Can't...hold back..."

Yet where would there ever be any need to hold back as he slammed into her cunt, gasping through breathy howls, a dog so far beyond anything in anthro worlds of civilisation that he may as well have been nothing more than a feral brute. The malamute shuddered, giving one last howl, spending his seed inside her. He too did not knot her, ensuring that her cunt could be filled, a good load of slick cream flowing forth, some drooling out around his fat girth even as he slowed.

One cock would be traded for another, her maw left empty, lips open. She was ready, oh, she was. She had to have it and, that time, she caught sight of the foxhound who teased his cock between her lips. His cock was a little smaller but still a good size – not that she would have turned down any breeding pole in her state of complete and utter intoxicating lust. He was gentler than the others, but maybe that was as the motion of his hips came naturally to him, tail wagging, lingering in pleasure even as the third dog filled the vixen's pussy.

She tried to look up but she could not see him, only left imagining him as some kind of mutt, shaggy-haired and rough in his presentation. That was how it felt, at least, as he slammed into her, his paws on her hips, the light spark of pain from him putting too much of his weight on her still not enough to stop the vixen from taking it all. She would have done it too, strained around that massive length, the tip questing deeply up to her innermost barrier, but the bondage took that pleasure from her, giving her a new kind of ecstasy in its stead.

Orgasm ripped through her and, from that point, there was no telling where one orgasm ended and the next began for the breeding bitch. She was there to please the dogs and only the dogs, emptying load after load of virile cum into her cunt, the best of the best. She might have whined and whimpered to have her arse filled too but, alas, that time was merely for her to take their seed and impregnate her, her lower abdomen feeling oddly tight, as if she was swollen down there. That couldn't be possible though, surely?

"Such a bitch…"

"Fucking breeding whore…"

"My seed will win here."

"She'll be so fat with pups."

Dog pups, not even cubs. One dog was swapped for another, the foxhound taking his pleasure from her too in a series of short, sharp thrusts, wasting no time about using her body. He did pause, however, to wipe his dick off on the creamy fur of her abdomen, the vixen shivering. Why did something like that, even then, have to make her feel so good?

None of it made sense but it did not have to come with any true sense of clarity in a moment like that, three dogs surrounding her. While a Rottweiler ploughed into her gaping, drooling pussy, messy with cream-pie after cream-pie, a greyhound took her muzzle, living up to his racing name. The third dog, a lab-type crossbreed, made use of her tits, leaning over her body, however awkward the angle was, grinding his dick into the softly luscious, yielding flesh of her breasts.

It was too much sensation for one body to take and yet she was there for the long haul, the vixen's body an object of lust for the dogs. Her pussy squelched with every thrust of the Rottweiler's and she moaned around the dick in her mouth, only wanting their cum. If they gave her every last load that they had in their throbbing nuts to give she would be a very happy vixen indeed, even if there was only so much that her body could take, even when she was in heat. She would push herself to her limits and beyond, craving it desperately, cum dripping from her muzzle as the greyhound simply could not last, exploding in her maw and pouring his load down her throat.

She gulped and coughed, struggling to swallow at such an angle, the thick headiness of his cum filling her nose, her senses enveloped in the musk of his body. He didn't seem to much care that he'd cum too quickly, the lab-type taking his place, letting her tongue wrap around and caress his cock with a lusty moan rather than wasting energy in thrusting. Labs, after all, tended to be like that.

At least from the fox's experience.

"She can't last much longer."

"How much cum do you think that whore's cunt will take?"

Oh, everything, she wanted to tell them, but her maw was full. Everything you have to give and more: *try me*.

The Rottie slammed in, hips working like a piston, snarling and pulling his lips back from his teeth, although there was no one, really, there for him to challenge even in such a twisting exultation of passion. He grabbed her thighs and hunkered over her as if he could lift her up to meet his bone-shaking thrusts, but he still had to keep the thickening swell of his knot out of her cunt if he wanted to let the others ride her pussy too. It was hard, even harder with her sex flexing and tightening the best it could around him, though anything she managed to do in squeezing down was purely an erratic accident. She slurped the cock in her muzzle, body aching through yet another orgasm, electric thrills zinging forth, but pricked her ears still as the Rottweiler howled through the emptying of his balls into her sloppy pussy.

There was no longer any resistance in her pussy as another dog, an Irish wolfhound with a growl pulling at his lips, thrust into her. She hadn't even heard him come in, but it seemed that the Lab was more concerned with taking her muzzle than her cunt: she hardly cared as long as she was still well-bred at the end of it. In the meantime, until she passed out from sexual, blissful exhaustion, they could use her body however they pleased, whatever suited them.

Lust dragged at her, one moment blurring into the next, pleasure overcoming her. The tightness holding her limbs in place came with a deeper sort of ache from not being able to move and pulling so hard at them, even the bondage bench feeling stiff and unyielding through the padding. The Lab growled and grunted as he spent himself in her maw and she was better-prepared that time to tilt her muzzle, swallowing down all she could even if most slopped messily back out of her muzzle at such an angle. Still, she was marked by him as their breeding slut of the night and the vixen could let him go with satisfaction and the taste of him lingering on her lips.

But there was one stud left amongst the chaos of dogs, another shaft that she did not recognise slipping from her pussy without finishing, leaving the sloppy mess of her bred cunt for the master of them all. The Doberman rippled with muscle, walking with an easy roll to his gait, and she whimpered, knowing it was time. For if she'd thought that she had been stretched with their dicks so far, they would be nothing in comparison to the monster dick and fat knot that she was surely yet to take.

"This is where you belong, vixen, amongst the hounds."

His dominance set her moaning and she grunted, trying to arch up to meet him even as he speared into her. His heavy balls swung into her backside, slick and soaked with the seed of so many dogs, but that did not give the Doberman any pause at all as he pounded her, his paws resting and gripping either side of the bench's padding to lend the most force to his thrusts.

And he was thick, so very thick, stretching her open to such a point and demanding more as her body gave in to his easy dominance. Was that what it was to be controlled? It was no wonder that he went last, for her pussy would surely be stretched and useless if he had gone first, even if that was supposedly not to be the case. But that made her want him all the more, yowling and shrieking, letting her lust show as his massive cock set her exploding with orgasm all over again.

It was in the midst of orgasm that she felt him grasp her tits, claws digging in, pulling at and tweaking her nipples. She'd thought it was not possible for her climax to mount any more than in already had but it was too late for things like that to be questioned, need coursing through, her body on fire but simmering with cool at the same time. The cool of seed trickling over her, sweat soaking her fur, was too much to bear, slipping back and forth on the edge of consciousness, told her it was coming, though it was not as if she wanted to do a damn thing about it.

And, thus, the breeding gangbang came to a tumultuous close as he plunged his knot inside to swell, bellowing out his breeding lust for her, spending ropes after ropes of thick seed, trembling nuts pressed all the way up to her creamy backside. She shuddered in place, but it was for them to take in the moment, panting and heaving, passion coursing through, their lust something that would be remembered in the months to come and the swell of the vixen's belly. For truly, there had only ever been one stud dog's seed that could win out and that was the cum of the biggest and baddest mutt of them all.

Closing her eyes, she exhaled, the heat slipping from her body, just a little bit. When she woke again, her heat would have calmed. And she would be left with the bun in the oven she'd wanted all along.

What more could a slut like her want from a breeding gangbang?

Her lips stretched in a smile, exhaustion claiming her, as he pumped her pussy full.

# Carrying New Life

"Oh, my darling…"

He crooned, though the stallion should really have been taking care of his wife at that moment, even though Bryan was doing exactly that as he let her sit back against him on the sofa. Topless, the black sheen of his coat could be seen with not a spot of white on it – pure black all the way down to his hooves, mane spilling down the arch of his neck. Even though he was in his thirties, the stallion didn't have a hint of grey in his hair and could have passed for a younger horse.

He sat on the sofa while she perched on a thick cushion on the floor, her back to him, between his legs. Her long, golden mane spilt down her neck, though it was dyed and the roots needed doing again. Ida always lamented how much it cost to have a full, equine mane dyed at the salon, so he had said that, of course, he would do it for her next time, all so she didn't have to worry about any of that by herself. With the pregnancy coming, their focus had to be elsewhere.

But the horse couple understood that too as Ida leaned back against her husband and he massaged her shoulders, murmuring to her, wishing he could do more than simply rub her shoulders. If only he could take the burden part of the pregnancy away from her – then, maybe, Bryan would finally feel like he was doing enough for her. But things were not always that easy, even in the soft peace of their living room.

"My legs are so sore," she whinnied gently, leaning back against him. "Please… Can you rub them for me, sweety? I don't want to put you out?"

Bryan smiled, running his hands down her arms to her waist and across her large, round stomach, eight months pregnant and getting to the end of her pregnancy. He couldn't wait to welcome their little one into the world.

"I can do much more than that, darling," he nickered softly, green eyes brimming over with love for her. "Come up here, let me take care of you."

Of course, massaging her legs was brought into it, but Bryan had so much more in mind for her, helping her out of her clothes and her bra too, though her panties remained in place for the moment. Her body had become softer and curvier with her pregnancy, but that was not a bad thing in the slightest, not when he could adore even more of her. After all, the gorgeous bay mare was carrying their foal and he could only dote on her.

His hands expertly slid over her, easing away tension from her muscles, down her arms, soothing her shoulders, working down around her belly too. That was something that Bryan had seen online, about giving a pregnancy massage, but he could only hope he was doing the right thing as his wife moaned.

"Oh, Bryan…"

"Shush, let me take care of you."

Afterwards, he would make her dinner and ensure that the mare had everything that she could possibly want, but that moment was all about her. He kissed down over her stomach, parting her legs gently, though the stallion took a moment to slide her underwear down her legs too, right there in the living room, the TV on in the background and the lighting soft.

The rest of the world, however, fell away when he moved between her legs, his nose pressing up to her pussy, nuzzling, lapping. He knew the intricacies of her body better than anyone else, better than even he knew his own, and played that all to his advantage, especially when it was all worked towards her pleasure. The mare moaned and rocked her hips up to him as he grunted into her sex, his tail lifting, the velvety dock exposed. Sometimes, when they were playing together, they toyed a little with other parts of the body, the sensitivity of their docks something that some equines leaned into experimenting with, but that day was all about her.

He groaned, lavishing attention on her cunny, his tongue covering her folds in long, broad strokes, penetrating them softly, dipping into her pussy. He stroked up inside her, finding her G-spot easily, though Ida could not lift her legs as much as she could before to wrap around him. With her pregnant belly, she was even more beautiful to him, though that did mean that some things had to be set aside in lieu of that.

"Mmm… Oh!"

His wife groaned so beautifully that he couldn't help but continue, suckling on her clit, doing all the right little things that he knew would drive her insane with pleasure. It didn't have to be a slow build either, not after working out the kinks from her body with the massage, though he would spend some extra time and attention on her legs later, just for her. All for her.

For he could lose himself there, between her legs, swirling his thick, fleshy tongue around her clit, drawing it into his mouth and moaning, all so the soft vibrations from his lips would ease into her too, bit by bit. He couldn't help it, losing himself in the giving of pleasure, her pussy dripping even as he slipped two fingers into her. That was not enough for his wife when she was that aroused and wet, panting and trying to cling to his head. Her belly slightly got in the way, but Ida just about managed to get her hand down to twist her fingers into his forelock.

"Oh, yes… Ah! Bryan!"

She was close already and the stallion eagerly leaned into her, relishing in the soft feel of her thighs pressing in on either side of his head. He swirled his tongue around her clit, though his lips closing around it while he flicked his tongue rapidly over the nub of sensitive flesh was what did it for her, his fingers working deep to curl up against her G-spot. It had the mare grunting and panting, trying to arch up against him – all to the point where she couldn't possibly contain herself for a single moment longer.

Her cries of passion filled the living room even over the soft murmurs of the TV, though Bryan wasn't thinking about any of that. Sure, his cock had pushed out from his equine sheath, though he didn't let it loose, in his shorts, the room warm in the middle of summer. No, he could ignore that for the pleasure of his wife as she rode out her high on his muzzle, Ida's juices drooling down his face, trickling over his chin.

"Mm… Bryan… Please, come here, I need… I need you."

His ears pricked and he leaned his head against his wife's thigh, though Ida didn't want him to wait. With a needy whinny, she spread her legs even more for him, showing off the dripping mess of her pussy, so thick with her own arousal that it almost looked like he had cum inside her already. Yet that was exactly what the mare wanted, eyes on him, his crotch, mentally undressing him.

"Okay, my love, if that's what you…unff…want…"

It was hard to get his shorts and boxer briefs off with his shaft trying to make itself more and more known, but he had to, for her, even though his arousal was clearly up too. With the warmth of the air folding itself in around them, the stallion could only nicker with need, stomping lightly with a swish of his tail, finally freeing his erection as it sprang out before him. A dark grey length, there were some darker flecks of colour along the length, the tip flat and plumping up already, showing where there was still more of his shaft to thicken up, even then.

But he would be gentle with his wife, even as she drew him to her, more than able to still get what she wanted from him, despite her condition. Ida grinned to her husband with a flirtatious neigh and flick of her tail, turning around on the sofa so that she was sort of on all fours with her back to him, her hands up on the back of the sofa for balance and support. It meant that she did have to bear the weight of her stomach under her, but that was something the mare was willing to live with, having the freedom of movement instead.

"Please…" Ida groaned, casting him a seductive look back over her shoulder, tail flagged high and pushed wantonly off to the side. "I need you… Fill me, husband!"

Even though there was no breeding need for them to have that kind of sex with her pregnancy in full swing, it was all for a matter of closeness, of knowing the other was there for them. He pressed over her, the head of his shaft squeezing up against her pussy, already dripping pre-cum, but, well, that had always been a thing for Bryan. His dear mare nickered to him, but it was with a protective hand on her belly that he pushed into her, his shaft spreading her delicious, succulent folds apart.

Their moans filled the air and, just like that, the aches and pains of her pregnancy and the day fell away, Bryan holding her belly lightly with his hand as he rolled his hips, spearing into her, again and again. Every stroke brought with it a fresh wave of pleasure as he moaned, though the stallion was very much in control of himself, even though he felt like he was going to blow at any second. There simply was not anything that he could ever do to harm his wife, thinking of her pleasure above all else. Even if he did cum too quickly, he would only take his time finishing her off with his mouth and fingers, ensuring she always got what she deserved.

Yet that moment was not for Ida alone, but for both. She rocked her hips back at him, slowly and surely, matching his pace, though she didn't have the energy or the mobility to grind back any more roughly than that. He took charge for both of them, helping to support her as his arm went around her, drawing her in close, securely, every stroke pushing in the entirety of his cock. Bryan wouldn't do anything less than that as he filled her repeatedly, the skin of his shaft pulling lightly where the medial ring caught on her folds. It tugged and pulled, stimulating him even further, need coursing through, pump after pump sinking into her.

It was needed, so very much so, grunting thickly in the back of his throat. He longed for it and so did she, remembering that they loved and lusted for each other through everything, that they would always be together despite the changes to come in their life.

For it was together, once more, that they would climax, his cock throbbing and twitching inside her, closer and closer with every lustful stroke. He grunted and twisted his head back and forth, nearly close enough to push over her shoulder, though he didn't want to be too heavy for her, considering the load that she was carrying for them both.

Her nickers goaded him on to their joint high, however, whimpering, breathily pressing back against him, while her pussy contracted, rippling and pulling around him, milking him. The stallion could not hold back for a single moment longer, not as she tipped into orgasm, her pussy squeezing him so hard that he could not resist her, the lure of her body and her mind.

They lost themselves right there and then, together, his cock throbbing, the head flaring, thickening, spilling his thick, creamy load deep into her pussy. Every spurt sent a deeper wave of lust through him than the one that came before it, though he only thought of her, making sure that she had everything she wanted, everything she needed. His orgasm was only part of it, though Bryan did not realise, even then, that Ida was doing all she could to take care of his needs too.

He moaned, holding her close, seating them on the sofa, comfortably, her body tucked into the curve of his. His paw traced the curve of her belly as he groaned, though he kissed the back of her neck and her cheek tiredly, a soft smile easing across his lips. He held her close, stroking her belly, nuzzling into her neck, relaxing there, even though their legs were kicked off the sofa, meaning they would have to move, sooner or later. But, until then, they could relax in the afterglow, letting everything sink in, muscles soothed from orgasm.

With his wife glowing in pregnancy, there was nothing Bryan wouldn't do for her. But it was a good thing that Ida too was there for him, loving her husband as much, if not more, than he loved her.

# Tender Care

Warm summer nights were built for lust, tender kisses and touches beside the pool. The gryphons softly kissed, tilting their beaks so that they could lock them together, allowing them to kiss, though they had no lips that they could, more softly, mould to one another's mouths.

It was better that way, Symone divine in her rich, dark-brown fur and the black of her feathers, her beak a dark shade too, though it changed with the seasons. The tufts that were often mistaken for ears were long with her, able to be styled, though they were often unruly unless one used the right feather treatments with them. Her lover had shown her what to use, a midnight-blue gryphon with kind eyes and a light touch that made her feel as if he was flying, even when her claws were quite firmly on the ground.

Eli would take care of her, softening the troubles of a terrible year for hunting and family, the heatwave that had swept through and rendered their usual hunting grounds barren. The heat had eased, leaving them in a new territory, luscious and rich with thriving plant life, the last rays of sunset catching the bubbling pool where it was fed by a natural spring. High in the mountains, Eli and Symone would return to their flock when they were ready, but that was the best place for two feral gryphons to show one another just how deep their love ran, after so much time.

"Oh…"

Symone laid back beside the water, her beak tilted to the side, eyelids fluttering. It was not a natural position for a four-legged, feral gryphon to be in, on her back, but she wriggled and fluttered her wings out so that they were splayed, her belly rising with every shuddering breath. Yet her lover would never harm her as she watched his dark blue, feathered head make its way down her body, nibbling and kissing, showing her without the aid of any words at all how much he adored her.

And Eli did, giving his life for Symone, the richness to their coats and feathers showing one another how much they had prospered. For it was through the darkness that light came once more, his leonine tail lashing the air as he hungrily dove between her legs. On her back, they splayed out and could not be bent in a way that would have allowed her to brace against the ground, the soft, damp earth yielding to them. That left her body there to be devoured.

"Ohhhhh!"

Symone cried out his name, trying to cling to him, though her talons missed. Even if she had caught Eli's head, she would have most likely only pulled out tufts of feathers, his tongue delving up into her pussy, tasting her essence. It pulled against her folds deliciously, seeking out that spot inside her that made the gryphoness squirm and keen, though Eli would always see to it that she received the utmost pleasure from him. It was all he could do, all that he would ever do, always for her, only for her. She was the only gryphoness that he had ever been with, his first, the two of them long-time mates and they knew each other's bodies inside out, better than anyone ever could.

He growled playfully into her sex, his beak pressing a light indent into her vent, the slit under her tail hole where such pleasures were held. She'd never laid a clutch before, but, maybe, this time, this time would be the time that she "took", his shaft sliding out, hardening, balls hidden in a thick, dark fluff of fur between his hind legs. Even if they were not obvious, that did not mean that they were not there, his seed churning within, simply begging to be spilt.

With so much stress going on and rumbling, hungry bellies, the gryphons had not had the chance to lie together in such a way for a long time, something that Eli was keen to change as he slurped into her sex. His tongue sought out the pleasurable spots inside her, wriggling it out against her sensitive entrance, seeking the spot that had her squirming so wonderfully. It took him a few attempts, but the drake was persistent enough to find that patch of nerves that had her beak opening and closing soundlessly, crying out with no breath to do so, chest tight with need.

Yet it was her gryphon drake who would always sate and satisfy that need for her, always and forever. He nuzzled lovingly against her, inhaling her essence with needy breath after breath, Symone wriggling, panting, crying out his name.

"Oh… Eli… Eli… Yes… More…"

She didn't have the breath with which to tell him what she wanted from him, though she could wriggle and puff out air through the nares on her beak, head spinning with passion. Oh, it had been so long, but that was understandable, so very much so. She just needed it all, something tightening inside her body, her loins lurching even as her tail thrashed back and forth, passion mounting and mounting.

To be mounted, to be bred, to be fucked… It was rawer than mere sex and something more carnal, something she yearned for. Yet it was up to Eli to give her the sweetness, first of all, nuzzling and slurping into her pussy, lapping up her juices even as they squelched forth from her sex, beckoning him in. Even though his cock was hard, a long, smooth length with a defined head and a sharply tapered tip that was designed for softly penetrating and prying open a partner, he would not, not until she had enjoyed her fill first.

He'd always been like that. But, sometimes, all Symone wanted him to do was to fuck her and breed her like he never had done before.

Her body was for him, however, and Eli would do with it as he saw fit, greedily lapping into her, exploring her sex, her scent overwhelming him as he sucked in short, needy gasps. Her stomach tightened and tightened, contracting muscles that had not been used for such a purpose in months, a full stomach goading her on.

She was not hungry, she was with her mate, the world around them was prosperous: it was the right time to mate, her body told her. So, do it!

Symone panted, eyes wide, wriggling, fighting, the tension too much to bear at the peak, so close after what felt like only a few moments, but she could not honestly tell for how long Eli had been down there between her legs. It only felt as if it had been instant, time losing all meaning between them in the heat of a moment like that, the soothing bubbling of the pool nowhere near enough to cool the blast of their passions. But nothing had to be cooled as she keened out through undulating waves of ecstasy, the storm that she wanted to bear through crashing over her, pounding pulse after pulse setting her pussy rippling erratically. There was no rhythm to the pulses drawn from her body, muscles beyond her control, yet her lover lapped and lapped, slurping up her freely flowing juices as he helped her ride it out.

Only when she had softened into the afterglow did Eli help her to, very gently, turn over onto her stomach, willingly lifting her tail for him. The hard spire of his cock sought out her pussy as he pushed over her back, nuzzling at her head, kissing her beak, words shared only between them.

"I love you so much. I don't think I would have gotten through this last year if not for you."

Symone parted her beak to answer him, though all that slipped free was a shrill cry as he penetrated her with his thick length, the slender tip easing in and them spreading her sex open to accommodate him. Her pussy closed around him, tight but not too tight, the perfect tension to thrust, her juices easily lubricating the way for him while the drake could not produce his own lubricating moisture.

"Ah… Yes… Oh, Symone…" He moaned, losing himself, wings fluttering, tongue flickering out over the edge of his beak. "You feel…so good…"

And she did, her sex enveloping him as they embraced in the most intimate of ways, her body warm around him, pulling him deeper. She squeezed down around him as hard as she could, attempting to milk his shaft, though the pulses of her pussy were weak, something that would, once again, come with time and practice if it proved to be important to them. The intimacy of being together, his bare length sliding within her, was more than enough to them right then and there, her hips trying to push back against him even as Eli, softly and lovingly, pinned her in place.

An act of dominance, however light it was, Symone squirming for him, catching her breath, lungs shuddering as she raked it in. One orgasm would not be enough for her as she squeezed around him, trying to get him there, moment after moment stoking the fire of her need. Her skin prickled with heating tension, electric thrills pulsing through her veins as if she was flying through a lightning storm, need pounding her with more force than even his shaft. He was not being slow and steady about it either, knowing what she liked, even though there was a more loving, passionate edge to their mating than usual.

Eli took her furtively, cock driving deep, his hindquarters rounding down around her, needing only Symone and her rich, golden-brown body. The gryphoness trembled and keened under him, her wings splaying out, though he covered her protectively with his body as he mounted her, promising without the use of any words to protect her from all harm. It was all that he'd wanted to do, to give the gryphoness a life that she deserved, though the world had not been as kind to the two of them as it could have been.

But they would come through of it, all of it, with his cock driving deep, tasting her succulent sweetness, the gryphoness twisting, striving to hump back. It did not matter that she couldn't, only that the desire was there, her hips rising a fraction, groaning as he took her.

"Yes, yes... Eli..." Symone closed her eyes, panting through her nares, though her beak opened too. "I'm...ah...so close..."

Yet he would not have slowed anyway as he grunted and growled against the back of her neck, talons curling around her hind legs, holding her in place as his thrusts sped up. He was feral, he was power, he was going to take her roughly to their ultimate completion. The slap of his hips on her back end resounded through the clearing, even over the warble of the pool and spring, grunting, heaving, two bodies coming together in bliss as they were apt to do. And that was quite the case as she shrieked out her ecstasy, wings flapping, orgasm gripping her even as her mate lovingly nipped at the back of her neck.

Though not even Eli could or would hold back his cries as he unloaded behind her, the tension and tightness in his nuts needing to go somewhere, pummelling through him, driving through, hips sending his seed forth in short, sharp, juddering thrusts. He barely pulled back before thrusting back in, the smack of his hips on her flesh echoing, though her moan begged for more.

Sweet spurts of thick seed flowed forth, nothing to cover or protect his cock, though that was all more than alright between such long-time mates. It was as it was meant to be, only to be, all between them, Eli panting heavily, wings drooping, his breath stolen as he half collapsed over her back. It was there that he stayed as he spent every last drop of seed that he had been storing up for her, all for her, inside Symone's pussy. The folds of it held him tight as he relieved himself, crooning and nibbling, nudging and licking at the back of her neck.

Their love was as strong as ever, regardless of what they had gone through. Maybe even more so for the trials that they had faced.

Symone shivered, feathers ruffling.

"I love you, Eli.

"And I love you, Symone."

Together, always and forever. His cock throbbed inside her, seed flowing deep. In the coming months, she would lay her first clutch and they would raise their young together.

# The Condom Broke

Ellie grinned as her partner, a tall hare with silvery fur, swept her up in his arms, carrying her up the stairs of their small home bridal-style. Of course, their wedding had been a few years back but, well, that didn't stop him treating her like a queen. Sometimes, she wouldn't have minded if her hare partner treated her more roughly.

There was a difference between them, however, the tiger anthro a good head taller than the hare, even though his ears did cheat at giving him additional height too. She had the typical orange and black fur markings of a tiger, though not much of a creamy-white belly and chest, but she knew he would have recognised her anywhere.

"Mmm, Ellie..." Ada murmured, kissing her cheek as he laid her on the bed. "You've been teasing me all day..."

Ellie grinned, squirming on the bed, her skirt hitching up a little more over her hips. Her blouse was long and flowing, not really "teasing" material, though it had been what she was wearing under that which had proved very useful in getting her boyfriend all good and randy.

"Yeah, me? I've been teasing *you*?"

She wriggled a little more, bringing her paws up to her chest, the base of the collarbone, her tail sweeping back and forth across the bed. The hare's eyes followed the play of her tail, but she didn't need him distracted, no, not then. Everything was just a little game she was playing, all with Ada.

"Mm, yeah, you," he said, coming back to himself a little and cocking his head. "You know what you do to me, Ellie, don't you?"

The tiger smirked and shook her head, though, of course, she knew full well what Ada meant, the hare sliding his paws down her legs, the fur bare to his touch. She couldn't help but moan, spreading them a little wider for him, though not giving up everything entirely. Her lingerie, after all, was a treat for him to unwrap, bit by bit...

Ellie never would have wanted to let everything show all at once. But she could play things exactly as she wanted to, for the only furs who were important in that scenario were her and her boyfriend.

Ada took a breath that was shakier than the hare would have liked, pulling back a little to look her over. He liked to take his time with his charming tigress, even if she had made him sport a hard-on in an office meeting that day, forced to remain seated until it had softened. Perhaps, ultimately, that was his fault for checking his phone during the meeting, though Ada had faced a funny feeling, back then, that he had wanted to check his phone for something special. It was strange, in a good way, how he always seemed to catch just when Ellie was up to something.

And the tiger brightened up every room she was in, making things seem fresh and new again – even if it was his house they had moved into, the little start-up home he'd managed to scrape together the deposit for. It was in a good position for his work and meant little more to him than that, though it was Ellie who made it special for him.

That, however, was not quite the moment to be as sappy as all that, shaking his head slowly and allowing a lewder kind of smirk to pull at his lips.

"Hm... I don't quite want to take these off you yet..."

Ada murmured, tugging her lingerie to the side, exposing her folds lightly, though the underwear barely moved, hugging her body perfectly. The light lace grew sheer over her crotch, showing the creamy, white fur there, though Ada's tongue softly played out between the tiger's thighs as he lapped, slowly and surely.

"Ohhhh…"

Even if she had started the game between them, Ellie moaned, her toes curling delightfully as her tail swished back and forth. Oh, his tongue was good, so very good, knowing her body more intimately than, sometimes, she even felt she knew herself. His tongue traced the outline of her folds, acting as if they had all the time in the world – and yet there was a sense of urgency and haste there, his need flaring.

But it was playing back and forth with that very sultry need that lured her so, the predator "hunting" her prey, though it was all a tease and a game for her, nothing serious. Ellie sank into it, relaxing into the bed, the sheets and mattress lightly moulding to the shape of her body. Planting her hind paws into the bed, she did her best not to let her claws dig into the sheets (she really didn't want to have to buy a new set so soon) and rolled her hips up, the sensual pump and grind of her body rolling all the way through.

Ada's ears twitched as the hare struggled to keep up with her, although it was not anything they hadn't done before, not as warmth tingled through her body. Maybe Ellie should have paid more attention than that, struck by the sudden urge to fan her face with her paw, though she shook it off lightly, putting it from her mind.

It was fine, everything was definitely fine. Especially as his tongue lightly pressed in between her folds, teasing her with that lure of pressure. Yet the hare did not do more as he savoured her, returning to running his tongue up the full length of her folds, from base to tip, just catching the bud of her clit as he pressed down just a little harder.

"Mmmmm…"

Ellie hummed happily, the rumble of a purr building in the back of her throat. Oh, more, she was more... Yet the feline was just as intrigued by letting him do as he willed, curious as to where her sweet hare was to take her that time.

Ada's nose twitched, nuzzling in close, enraptured by the world between her thighs. Her fur may have been soft but there was plenty of lean, powerful muscle there too, her legs tightening lightly around his head as if to simply remind him of the power that lay there. Ada blinked, half-closing his eyes, hazy with desire.

It was easy to slip away down there, his tongue dipping between her folds once more with renewed determination, teasing and lapping. She was so sweet and he lapped deeper still, his tongue playing with her entrance, the sensitive nerve endings there, and dragging it back up over her clit, his tongue lightly pulling at her clitoral hood. It was only a light touch, but it had her shuddering around him, rocking and twitching her hips up to his tongue.

"Oh... Yes... Ah..."

She huffed out a hissing breath, groaning as she rocked her body with the touch of his tongue, the hare's ears twitching. Ada listened intently, his tail twitching, though even flicking it up to reveal the soft, white underside was not sending any signals in the moment. Electric tingles ran through the hare, groaning as he buried his muzzle more firmly between her thighs, his fingers coming up to spread her pussy gently so he could get in even closer.

It was definitely where he needed to be, something luring and keeping the hare there as he groaned and pleased her, working the cat's body up more and more. The world outside their bedroom didn't matter and Ada would have been hard-pressed indeed to even remember what he'd been doing that day at work. The tiger simply had a way of sweeping things from his mind, as if she was so dominant in his life that her light and brightness illuminated absolutely everything he needed to focus on.

And the hare would not have minded in the slightest if all his attention was to be spent on her, until the end of his days. There could be no better way to spend his time, breath huffing and panting warmly over her inner thighs and pussy, though his sheath filled out increasingly with the soft rise of his cock. It was not much of a sheath, for a hare, more a small, plump tuck of flesh that lay close to his body, protecting his shaft when it was retracted and cradled within his body. His balls were bigger and more obvious though, fat and full with the need to seed – and what they joked about with bunnies was certainly true of hares as well.

His shaft eased out, a moderate girth that rose to eight inches long, showing his species just a little more. He'd wondered, long ago, if Ellie may have wanted a tiger with their barbed cocks (even if the barbs were softer and more pliable in the case of most anthros, not designed to cause pain even if they still could stimulate ovulation) but he had been more than enough for her. Even if Ellie had not said that clearly to him, her moans told the truth of the tale and her pleasure.

The tiger's thighs squeezed around him, hips bucking up, the hare blinking as he noticed an ache in his neck.

"Mmm, come here."

He blinked, startled by her pulling away – had he caught a sore spot or something? Yet the tiger growled with a gleam in her eye as he looked up the lean length of her body, the hare shivering in place.

"Mm, yes?"

But his tiger was quicker than him, squirming agilely down the length of the bed to pull him all the way up with her, in a better position for them both to enjoy one another. She rolled him on to his back, trapping his lips in a hungry kiss, the frenzied, rough nature of the kiss coming with a more dominant edge than what Elle would usually have pulled out.

She needed him, more than she ever had before, though the tigress could not put a reason to that, no. She could only kiss him, devouring and claiming his mouth with hers, her tongue lashing playfully into his mouth and forcing his own tongue back, making room for her.

"Mmmm…"

Ellie groaned into the kiss, though she ached for something, shifting down his body and breaking the kiss with a mutter on her lips. She didn't know what she wanted, only that there was need rolling through her, her skin shivering all over, though she couldn't visibly see it: it was as if she could only feel the vibrations for herself, just like that.

"Unff…"

Ah, that was it… She splayed her paw out on his chest and worked her way down, scratching her claws lightly through his fur as the silvery hare moaned and trembled beneath her. Yet Ellie's attention was on the treat of his cock as she lusciously captured it between her lips, closing them tightly around the head and suckling faintly.

Her groan rolled into him and she shuddered bodily, relishing in the feedback from him, the little twitches of his body and how he rocked up to her touch. But it was the tiger who was in control, no one else, dipping her muzzle to take the full length of his cock sensually into her mouth, her tongue cradling the underside.

That was something she had to be ever so slightly careful of too, her tongue rougher than those of most prey species. It was not rough enough, like some ancestors, to do what they needed when they were still hunting in the wild, but it was still unpleasant if she dragged it too forcefully against his cock.

So, she merely used her lips and the slide of them, up and down the full length of his aching prick, to please her hare, all while she savoured every inch of Ada she could. The hare was spectacular, lean and athletic, a spring literally in his step.

And the tigress adored just how easy he was to tease and please, to get worked up for her. It was more fun than ever to send him flirty, dirty photos of herself, never quite knowing what reaction she'd get – but the tigress could be certain it would be a positive reaction, regardless of how all quite played out.

"Mmmph, Ellie… Mm… So good…"

The hare's head swam with desire as she sucked his cock, bobbing her head, mimicking how he so longed to plunge into her wet pussy. The scent of sex and the light, natural aromas of their bodies mingled in the air, though he could barely think straight as she brought a tingling rise to his hard-on.

It would have been so easy to buck up into her mouth and thrust right then and there, yet the brimming lure of submission, however light it was, proved dominant in that moment, ironically so. He just wanted to see what she had for him, where his tigress would lead him, though with all the heat rushing to his member, Ada didn't know how long he was going to last, not at that time.

Things had to come, however, and he twitched and moaned, his hips rocking and juddering very faintly, though he didn't thrust up, no. He had to last longer, not yet wanting to cum in her mouth. They didn't use a condom for oral but his eyes slid to the bedside table where he knew a pack of fresh condoms lay in the drawer, ready and waiting for them.

He grunted, licking his lips as a ripple ran through his whole body. The deep ache played into his core, watching his tigress' lips slide up and down his cock, caressing his length, suckling on the tip as if Ellie really was trying to get him to cum at once. But he held back, trying to cast his mind to other matters, even as the fall of her breasts, cradled by that so very seductive lingerie, tried to break his resolve.

Yet he won out, even as she pulled off his cock again, licking her lips, her fingers curling possessively around the base as if to suggest she had something more in store for him, even then.

"I want you inside me," she purred, her tone leaving no question there for him to answer, not in the slightest. "Now."

The hare was extremely glad to oblige, though his tigress presented herself to him, that time, on all fours, flipping her tail out of the way. With a trick left to play, Ada grinned, taking her underwear between his teeth and dragging them down her thigh, pulling the near sheer fabric down and down and down. He could only get her panties, roughly, down to her knees as the tiger squirmed and protested before he had to use his paws, but it was still enough to toy with her need, to work her up more and more and more.

The hare smirked lightly as he used his paws to get her panties the rest of the way off, not caring one bit. She just had to stay still and sort of lift her knees, helping him ease them off, bit by bit. Her underwear caught on her right ankle but he managed it anyway, licking his lips as he slid his paws up Ellie's legs until dug faintly into the soft flesh of her backside. With Ada's thumbs pointing in towards her pussy, he pulled her sex apart softly with a light moan, shifting his weight, her pink folds glistening with her arousal.

He couldn't wait to be inside her, thumbing her clit lightly as the tiger hissed and swished her tail.

"Hurry…"

Ada, however, had to take a moment to grab a condom, not wanting to forget that at the moment it mattered. Sure, they'd used the contraceptive pill before, but she was on a break from it, since she'd struggled to adjust to a change in it.

He tore the condom wrapper with his teeth and handled it with a single paw, sliding it down over his cock with practised ease. Ada supposed that was one benefit to using condoms more regularly: he was fairly well-practised to getting it on with no fuss. Still, the smooth pull of the condom over his cock had him shivering, sensations a little dulled – though it was worth it, of course, to be safe.

Ada wasn't all that sure why they were trying to be safe anymore, not after they'd been together for so long… But in the middle of sex was not quite the time to be considering big changes in their life.

Later, maybe.

"Mmph, Ada, hurry, please!"

He'd never seen her that needy before, but she didn't seem to be all that off, so he shrugged off the unusual sensation and eased between her thighs, his cock pressed up to her sex. Yet before the hare could slide his achingly hard length into her pussy, she ground back on him, taking the first couple of inches, rather sharply, into her soaked sex.

The tigress moaned, though she was not even in her right mind enough to savour the feel of him inside her, her pussy clenching and pulling around him, as if she was trying to milk him of his seed, even in that moment. But he thrust harder, powering into her, and she didn't have to worry about what wanted or not, not then. Every stroke ploughed deep, his paws gripping her hips, and she shuddered under his suddenly more forceful thrusts, her tail lashing back against his chest.

"Ah, yes! Mmm… Harder, Ada, harder…"

He moaned throatily and her need rose, her pussy so tight around him. Did Ada feel bigger than usual? She didn't know how to consider that, though there was something different about them that day, even as her hare's shaking paws tugged at the back of her bra, struggling with the clasp.

Ellie moaned, grinding back, a ripple running through her as she squeezed around him, gasping faintly. He filled her perfectly, his cock hitting all the right spots inside her. She hated saying it, even in the privacy of her own head, but it felt like her pussy was on fire, her whole body burning up from the inside out, claws flexing without conscious thought and pulling into the blanket.

Ada shuddered to her back, hips juddering all the way up to her backside.

"Ellie…" He groaned, seeming to take a very long time to get his words out. "Are you… It kind of feels like… you're in heat?"

"Mmmm…" She groaned. "No…  No, I can't be… It's not quite… yet?"

But that was not so, in fact. For the tiger had miscalculated the number of weeks since her last cycle, though she could be glad in her case that it was not as if she had to deal with it every month. Her cycles were longer, though it made her heats more difficult to predict.

"Ah…" She groaned, arching her back to grind back even more desperately on to his cock, that hot length of meat throbbing inside her. "Fuck… Mmm… Damn it…"

She moaned, ears twitching, tail swinging back and forth against her partner. Having a condom on, of course, meant they didn't have to worry about her getting pregnant, though there was an issue to be had there too as she moaned, need rolling through her even more stringently than before as she relished in the driving throb and push of his cock.

Oh, but she wanted to feel more, his cock aching inside her, bare, flesh on flesh. Ellie swore she could still taste him in her mouth, the hint of his musk clinging to the back of her throat, panting heavily, her head swimming with that lure of desire.

"It's okay, Ellie, it's okay, ngghh…" He groaned, rubbing her hips, thrusting harder. "I've got you. I'll do this for you…as much as you need to get through it."

And that sounded like a very good idea indeed, her pussy clenching around him as the hare powered into her with short, jackhammer-like thrusts, just what his species was known for. Her whole body vibrated faintly with the force of his strokes and she moaned open-mouthed, her tongue pushing out softly against the teeth of her lower jaw, brushing her lip.

Ellie didn't think what the hare offered was possible, but there were other ways to deal with a heat too, of course. Pills and some herbal tinctures helped suppress it, for it would be difficult for females, males and others also to go about even the mundane aspects of daily life if there were no ways to mitigate the effects. But that did not mean it was not exquisite to relish in every driving pound of his cock inside her. He felt thicker than usual, or maybe that was her cunny, pulling around him, rippling and tightening, giving her a richer, fuller sense of friction than, honestly, Ellie thought she'd ever had before during sex.

Orgasm hit her unexpectedly, her claws sinking deep into the mattress, not only the sheets, as she groaned and slammed her hips back. Oh, how she wanted every inch of him inside her – but she wanted him to keep thrusting too! The tigress couldn't have it both ways, not even as Ada trembled against her, shifting his hips back and forth, though only slightly, grinding his weight into her hind end.

He stayed deep, thrusting more shortly and sharply than before, though he didn't pull back all that much. It was fortunate for him that the condom, even if only a little, dulled sensation for him, though more and more of the tiger's warmth flooded his body, seeping into him through his member. The hare's hips wiggled, nose twitching, and he helped her ride out her orgasm, marvelling at the fact she hadn't even needed any clitoral stimulation to tip over the edge. For Ellie, that was far from normal.

She growled and he trembled in turn, following the lead of her body as he thrust again, though something felt a little different. Like his cock was warmer than before, though he didn't quite feel like he was at the point of orgasm yet. No, he could hold back, his balls swinging and bouncing against her backside with every slow, deep thrust, using the full length of his cock to fill her cunny.

The repetitive motion didn't take all that much brainpower for him to grind in deep, no, not in the slightest, allowing him to sink into the moment just a little more. He licked his lips, savouring every thrust, though his eyes raked the body of the naked tigress under him.

Well, almost naked, for her breasts were still trapped by her bra and he gently unhooked it at the back for her without pausing in his slow thrusts. It eased from her shoulders but hung there, the tigress apparently not in her right mind enough, not right then, to lift one paw to get it at least halfway, or most of the way, off her body.

The muscles in her back bunched and pulled as she groaned and rolled her shoulders back, her shoulder blades growing a little more defined as she settled back into place, breath huffing and puffing, catching in her chest. The tiger shifted her weight, letting her chest tip down to the bed and push her backside up against him, the deeper, rougher angle searing through him like wildfire.

"Oh… Ellie… You're going to make me cum so quickly…"

"Mmm, yes…" She panted, her forearms flat to the bed. "Please, fill me…"

Of course, that was not really possible when he was driving into her with a condom, but it was nice to fantasise. It was nice for her to think about him spending his seed inside her, that thick rush of cream seeding new life, all set to grow within the soft cradle of her womb. She clenched around him with a throaty mewl that didn't sound at all like her, the tigress ripping up more of the sheets and mattress. In that way, she didn't even know what she was doing.

And yet it was not up to Ellie to hold back as she savoured it all, letting every sensation sink into her, her nose twitching faintly. There was still a lingering scent from his aftershave about the hare, or maybe that was just Ellie's sense of smell growing more poignant in the moment. She didn't really know what her heat could do when she went to such efforts to suppress it and make sure it never caused her a problem at work.

That moan left her breathily, the sensation of her partner ground up flush to her backside sensual, sharing body heat to the point they were one and the same. There was no difference there, though Ada's paw slipped around to the front of her pussy, rubbing her clit, and she bucked into his paw, arching her back, as if called by a higher power.

"Mmmm, Ada…"

He loved the sound of his name on her lips, though the hare wanted more, ached for more. Things still felt different and he made a vague mental note to see if she was up for sex next time her heat came around too, for he wanted to see if anything was different there too, if their sex could be even better than it was already. Sure, they played around with sex toys and experimented as much as they could with each other, trying out new tips and tricks and challenges, but he had not known it could all be as sultry as it was with her wet heat wrapped around him.

*Wait…*

Yet Ada could not wait, not as that familiar surge rose inside him, his need throbbing and aching. He rammed inside roughly, cramming every last inch of his cock into her pussy as if it was the only thing on his mind, gasping and heaving, ragged breaths clawing their way down his windpipe into his lungs.

And nothing compared to that moment of climax, not as he spent his seed, ecstasy rushing upon him as if it was filling him up from the toes to the tips of his ears, warmth flooding his body. Yet it was too late for the hare to hold back or even come to the realisation something was different, that things had changed in a way they could never take back. Not as the hare stayed there, his entire length buried in her pussy, succulently deep, panting as he unloaded his cream.

"Mmmm, Ellie," he breathed, barely able to get the words out, though that didn't matter in the heat of the moment, not when tenderness brought them even closer together than before. "I love you so much…"

As the waves of orgasm died down, he trembled, withdrawing his cock slowly. The hare's eyes widened as his cock emerged, the condom slick with her arousal until…the bare head emerged.

"Ah… Ellie!"

Ada groaned, shuddering, his ears ramrod straight. His tigress shifted under him, rolling on to her back, as he stared down at the condom, which was by no means hiding his cock from view, the cool air of the bedroom tickling the exposed head.

"What's up?"

"Ellie… It's torn!"

The condom had more than torn, yet the tiger didn't seem to be all that concerned, not on the outside anyway. Her tail flicked back and forth across the bed, brushing his thighs, as the hare slipped the condom off, where it had pretty much looked like it was ringing his shaft only, from below the head to the very base of his cock. There had been nothing there to stop his seed from flooding into her pussy as it was, balls aching, the thrum of desire still curling and pooling in his belly.

"Oh… That's too bad…" She chuckled, rubbing her forehead. "Sorry, still giddy… Still need you…"

Ada trembled.

"Uh… Are you okay? This could be bad."

She smiled and shook her head, though Ellie would later tell him that her heart rate had increased, that there was a flutter in her chest that had not been there before.

"Yes…" She had to be honest with him. "I mean… Okay, it's not ideal, but we were trying to be careful. I'll go take a morning-after pill and things will be okay. With you being a hare and me being a tiger, it's unlikely to result in anything."

He exhaled, puffing out his cheeks with air.

"Yeah… Yeah, I know, I guess," he said, chuckling as a rush of half-relief seeped through him. "Ah… Damn, that was… Ah, a real… You okay?"

"Yes, darling, yes, of course, I'm okay."

She reassured him softly, drawing him down to the bed with kisses, though Ellie took a moment to slip out of her bra. With no condom and no underwear, there was no longer anything at all to bar their naked bodies from reaching one another, lust rising once more, his shaft slowly but surely hardening all over again against her hip. The hare squirmed, but she held him to her, eyes gleaming when she finally allowed him to break the kiss, the faintest string of saliva connecting their lips for the briefest of moments.

Yet even those brief moments felt as if they stretched out into eternity as she moaned his name, spreading her legs a little more for him, her hare resting on top of her.

"I want you," she breathed. "We can take the risk, the condom already broke…"

Ada quivered, a faint smile on his lips.

"We can handle it if anything does happen," he said, though it was a decision they both had to make together, for there was no other way for things to go forward from there. "We've been together…for years."

She purred and rubbed her face into him. Even then, Ellie didn't realise she was leaning more into instinct, scent marking him as hers.

"Yeah… Everything is okay. There's nothing to worry about and I'll take care of any potential problems," she assured him breathily, "first thing in the morning."

It was a conversation, perhaps, they should have spent a little more time having, though there was nothing truly, not really, for them to worry about, breath shuddering in their chests as Ada's lips crashed back into hers. Sure, they had agreed, though he moaned almost desperately into the kiss, his cock throbbing and twitching very faintly, back to full, aching hardness despite only cumming a short while ago.

Oh, his cat was hot, so very hot. There was something exciting, even to him, about the moment having gone wrong, her breasts brushing his chest as he slowly got himself into position, pinning her thighs to the bed with his own in a mating press. They were forced a little apart, though not so far apart they were spread, moaning into the messy, sloppy kiss, their tongues battling back and forth between their mouths. There was no single one between them who was dominant, however, toying with power as it tingled and called to them.

Yet there was no power to be had as they took the risk and he slid into her for a second time, his cock achingly sensitive. Ada shouldn't have been that desperate, considering how recently he had orgasmed, yet the hare could not control himself, not when his tiger wanted him so badly.

"Oh, fuck…"

The hare moaned as he thrust fully into her, letting her pussy wrap him bare for the first time in… Well, it had been a long time. And he regretted very much not being able to find another alternative, to get that feeling all over again, huffing and panting as he thrust, his body finding a rhythm that suited him quickly enough.

"Mmm, you feel amazing," he breathed, his lips against hers, not really kissing but ready to do so if the moment called for it. "So hot… So tight… Divine… I love you so much. So, so much…"

"I love you too…ah…Ada… Always… I'll always love you… Nnff…"

She groaned, rocking her hips lightly up, though the position was the most forceful one her partner had put her in as yet, her body tingling with arousal. She liked it, mentally putting that note away for later, as he drove into her, a long, deep rhythm calling to something that lay fathoms inside her. It was all she needed, panting softly, focusing all her energy on dragging enough air into her lungs, just to stay in position, right where she wanted to be.

To be pinned like that was another sensation entirely and she took a agency back into her own paws as she raked her claws down his back, purring throatily. It was good to have him inside her, their bodies touching, fur-on-fur, desire coursing through. Yet she needed something more, the hot rush of his seed flowing up inside her all over again, grunting in the back of his throat as his eyes met hers, shining with adoration.

The condom may have broken, though she knew with no shadow of a doubt that all was well, that all would come out as it was meant to. She took him deep, the plunging, trembling thrust of his cock rolling through her, even if she could not rock her hips up to meet him as she might have liked to do.

Yet he gave her everything she needed, even if they were both taking a risk, plunging his cock into her over and over again, filling her to the brim. The position made her pussy so much tighter around his cock than it had been before and she gasped, letting him kiss and nibble at her neck while she settled on his rump, digging her claws into him.

The hare muttered under his breath, a curse on his lips, powering in as he neared his high. It was impossible for Ada to tell how much time had passed, his need flaring, balls swinging back and forth lightly to brush her furred rump. The tiger's tail swished, calling him to the present moment, and he grunted throatily, relishing in every thrust, even if he could not commit every second of the whole experience to memory as he wanted.

That would have to come in the future, as he fucked his partner through her pregnancy – and, yes, made love to her too. For there was more than enough room in their relationship for both kinds of sex, yes, of course, her orgasm clawing at him, pussy tightening, and driving him too over the edge.

He howled, matching her yowl, his cock buried fully inside her, right up to the base, as they shared their orgasm. Ecstasy rolled through him, that wicked sense of knowing there was nothing barring his cock from her soft, sensual flesh easing deep into his body. He cried out, a broken, strangled gasp, yet the hare too was right where he wanted to be, moaning, staying there, his teeth on her neck, suckling softly, while they took the moment and made it their own.

They'd remember that night, of course, when the positive pregnancy test (and the subsequent ones) was checked and when her belly swelled with sweet new life. But it had been their risk to take and something they had done with the full knowledge of what they were doing, as adults, even if Ellie's heat had swayed them ever so slightly.

Such was life – and the beauty of it. Everything was as it needed to be as they nestled close in the afterglow, the hare's cock twitching faintly inside her as it spent the last dribbles of his seed right up where it belonged.

The condom may have broken, but, in the process, they created something new.

# Rainy Day Lust

## Part One

"Is it ever going to stop raining?"

Sitting in the entrance of the cave, Gael sighed, the white-feathered gryphon flopping down in as dramatic a fashion as his, somewhat scruffy, four-legged body was able to. Grunting, he rolled and wriggled onto his back, flicking his tail, the furred half of his body a darker shade of grey that stood out in contrast to the pure white of his feathers. There was little innocent about the young male, however, an adult in every right even though he still lived fairly close to the nest of his parental figures. Sometimes, in more ways than one, it proved somewhat difficult to get the not so little hatchlings to fly the nest, as it was.

But it was fortunate that Gael, at least, had some company on a day where a grey swathe of blustery rain swept through the mountains, turning the shockingly rugged, stark landscape into something all the more foreboding still. Whereas it was a treacherous landscape at the best of times, it became all the more tumultuous when the storms rolled in and it was not even exciting when there was no thunder and lightning to go along with it, bringing a rise and a bristle to both his feathers and his hackles. His friend since hatching, from another clutch of eggs, laid further back in the cave away from the mouth, which was at great and ever-increasing risk of becoming damp, chewing carefully on a bone that had been bleached white by the sun in drier times.

A little smaller than Gael, Miya could not be said to have a single feather or hair out of place on her body, perfectly groomed at all times. It made complete sense that the golden-brown gryphon, reminiscent of a traditional golden eagle and the olden feral gryphons of times long gone by, did not enjoy getting wet to say the least as that would have detracted from her good lucks, even though she was a formidable solo hunter too.

She'd returned before any of the others in her clutch with blood staining her beak and a gleam in her amber eyes that promised more, despite the fact that she'd, of course, had to wash herself off in the stream immediately. Hunting did not mean that she didn't have to take care of her own personal hygiene and cleanliness, after all, and it was a trait she carried along with her through her teenage years into adulthood.

And that was just why she spent so much time with that old bone too, chewing and working away, carefully and patiently, at the edges of her beak. The sides did not need to be sharp for what a gryphon needed from life but there was a fine art to grinding the hooked tip into a wicked point – something that other gryphons found very attractive in a mate, it was said. Gael would not have been able to say anything about that one way or another, however, as he didn't really see much of anything in gryphon hens as yet, except for the one friend who had, somehow, maintained her patience with him all through the groans and grumbles and angst of his teenage years.

It was only a shame that the whining had continued into adulthood too…

"Miya? Miya, are you even *listening* to me?"

"I've heard you complain about the weather a thousand times over," she said with a roll of her eyes, barely looking up still. "One more time will not ruffle my feathers, Gael. Why don't you carve or something?"

She inclined her head to the stone blocks at the back of the cave, something considered a typical and intriguing hobby for the enlightened gryphons. It was not unlike their kind in times where prey was plentiful and the race for survival hardly so at all to find other pursuits to occupy them, particularly with humans coming closer and closer to their territories, cities expanding. They picked up influences even from passing traders and curiosities as gryphons were as like as dragons were to hoard treasure. It was uncouth to compare gryphons to dragons, however.

But Gael shook his head, sitting up and tucking his front paws together, the talons touching.

"No... No, I've spent hours doing that."

Miya sighed, putting her bone aside at last, her dark grey beak gleaming, smooth where she wanted it to be and sharp in just the right spot. Perfect.

"And I'm sure you only want to sprawl in the sun right now, hm, don't you? Gael, why do you always want what you can't have?"

He sat up a little straighter while pulling his head and neck back in closer to his body, hunching even as the tension in his spine set him taller.

"I... Well... It's..."

And yet that was a question that the mature gryphon drake would never be able to answer, shifting his weight uncomfortably as he all but deflated in a hefty sigh that Miya would have sworn could have woken the dead. He made a show of everything even without thinking about it, making it impossible to not consider him being in the same location regardless of whether they were outdoors or tucked away, safe and dry, in a cave. Her heart pulled for him just a little but it was difficult to feel *too* sorry for him when there wasn't really anything wrong at all.

Ah, but the reasons why she stayed around him ran deep in the sensation of his fur and feathers pressed up against her on a cold, winter night, sharing one abode most of the time even when they could have retreated to separate sleeping quarters. The tremor in his muscles at full-blooded flight, outstretched for that extra burst of speed, made her heart pound and, if the muscles in her face had allowed it, she would even have given a shy smile. And Miya was not a gryphon hen who was at all predisposed to shyness even if she still was very much striving to learn all she could, to understand the strange feelings and needs rising up inside her, why she was so attached to this one drake who, really, could have been any other.

But…he was not. He could never be another gryphon and she watched him obviously, not showing a single drop of shame in her stare. He shuffled and eyed her in turn but, for gryphons, eye contact was not intimidating in its normal state; it took a very specific manner of hunting stare to draw an expression into discomfort. They could look all they liked and all would be well, but it was Miya's eyes that drew hungry, needy lines over the curves of his body, where the muscle stood out through fur as if he was posing there, just for her.

*Only* for her. That was it, was it not?

"What?" Gael said at last, breaking the silence that was already broken by the constant patter and stream of rain pouring from the lip that overhung the cave mouth. "What is it? I'll be quiet… I just really wanted to go down to the lake today."

Ah, the lake. That was a place that she remembered and knew well, although for likely different reasons to Gael. Miya clicked the edges of her beak lightly together in a gryphon purr. That had been a good day and maybe the first day that she'd really looked at Gael in a different light. She'd seen him as an adult stud gryphon drake for the first time that day when he'd dunked her under the water and she'd come up in a spluttering mess of feathers and shattered water droplets – all just to find him hovering over her with his beak parted in a gryphon grin. The water had flattened down his fur to his body, defining every last bulge of muscle, and her jaw had dropped for long enough for him to get ahead of her again and shove her beneath the surface with a childish crow of giddy joy.

He was there and so was she. And, so…why was it so difficult for them to come together? She shook her head at him, standing and stretching out one leg after the other, her tail curling back and forth quietly, thoughtfully. Maybe, just maybe, that was one instance where Miya simply could not wait for a gryphon drake to take the lead, the need for more curling in her gut, a tightening of muscles that could not be ignored. Every hen, she knew, would have a need to breed and bear eggs, although it came to each and every one of them at different times. It seemed that for her, however, the desire for eggs and caring for a clutch had come to an earlier time.

So, why fight it? Preening carefully, she eyed him, not hiding her interest, holding raw tension in her shoulders, right at the base of her large, glorious wings that she usually kept tucked in close to her back. But, in that moment, they spread slowly, each and every feather trembling as if they had come alive, defined in their resilience to her changing body. Every gryphon, in the end, had to grow up at some point and it seemed that Miya had mentally and emotionally matured at a swifter rate than Gael. That did not mean, to her, that he would not or even could not come along on the journey with her. She just had to take the lead and since when had that been at all a strange concept to her?

Smiling softly, the muscles around her eyes relaxing, she stood and stretched out her forelegs as if she was bowing down in play, although that was not a motion that she'd performed for many, many years. Somehow, however, it felt right and she released the stretch with a groan of satisfaction, tail swishing back and forth sinuously in time with the sway of her hips, eyes bright and eager for what she now knew that she needed. How it could have ever bypassed her attention was beyond her as her skin burned, although she was far from a dragon with an inner heat, the fire within licking at their scales on a constant, minute by minute, basis. Yet Miya did not need to understand every last eccentricity and nuance in her heart and soul, panting lightly as she advanced, knowing, at long last, just what she needed to do.

Closer and closer... Gael stepped back from her, his back arched and eyes wary.

"Miya? What are you doing?"

He may not have understood just what was going on but, ah, there was something more there that the drake knew of, the predatory gleam in her eyes that meant more, so very much more. Yet the hunt that she was on would not end in a kill but a life as she gave the gryphon approximation of a smirk, hunkering down a little lower to the ground in as playful a stalk as her lusty body could imagine.

"I know you're bored, Gael, I do understand."

Soothing, so very soothing. Her words slipped over him like water trickling down a crevice, drawing one's attention to just how the light glanced off it, teasing pleasures untold. There was always more than met the eye and he could no longer take things at face value, drawing in a sharp, short breath through his nares, the orbs of his daring, blue eyes as round and stark as they ever had been. Yet having one's eyes wide open did not mean that he was seeing as she purred and bumped her beak lightly against his, a show of affection that a drake like him could not have, truly, have expected.

"Miya..."

"Yes?"

Ah, but, no, he was not there yet and she tucked her beak under his chin, every nerve-ending in her body tingling, a line of tension crickling and crackling down her spine as if she was working out the kinks over and over again. Gael panted lightly in turn, not knowing or understanding, yet there was nowhere left for him to go but out into the rain, the storm growling at his back as if it was there too to force him into her needy paws. But Miya had no qualm or worry about the drake making a break for it, for she must have always had him where she'd wanted him – it had only taken one of them to come to that realisation at some point to move things along to the very next level for the two of them. And there was only one way to go in flight that Miya loved and that was *up*.

"What… What are you doing, Miya?" He asked, but something must have twisted in Gael's gut too as his words came out with a husky hue, rougher and coarser than before. "What is this about? I didn't mean…"

And yet there were not the words to convey what instinct knew was going to occur, what his body and his mind craved without knowing what he was charging towards, a feathered mass of writhing muscle that could only ruffle into the fray with ungainly youth. But that was alright when both of them were as grown as the other, their close proximity lending a sense of softening familiarity that, at the very least, took the rise out of his hackles.

"I think you *know* what I want, what we want. And, Gael, would I really want you to be so bored for even a moment longer? I have something for you… We could…"

Giggling, Miya fluttered her eyelashes at him – surprisingly long and flirtatious for a gryphon. But Gael didn't realise what she was insinuating where a more experienced gryphon may have taken the bait or, at the very least, understood her proposition. Yet she was a hen who was interested in the ways of gryphons coming together as one being, creating life, while he was a drake who was most likely more interested in flying fast and catching a bigger deer than he had on his last hunt, forever trying to outdo his self of the last time and the time before that.

She rubbed against him, teasing the sinuous, flexible length of her body down against his as he churred unknowingly in the back of his throat, the edges of his beak grinding lightly together. Miya would indeed have to take the lead but that was alright too as she nuzzled down his body, exploring and grooming his fur in more intimate, sensual detail than she ever had done before. It was far more carnal and softening to be so close to him, taking in his body before the might of the storm and not for the first time she rang flush with gratitude that, after everything that could have sent them on different flights in life, they had stayed together. Maybe, regardless of the tumultuous nature of gryphon relationships and the twists and turns of life, they had always been meant to be together.

Down and lower, she eased around under his stomach, lying on the cave floor as she chuckled softly, throatily, to herself, tail lashing all the while. Not anxious in the slightest, she eagerly anticipated what was to come and sent out a quick prayer of thanks to the gryphon hens of flocks nearby that had taught her and told her what to expect from a mating, even if it was something that every hen would have to come to herself. Once it began too, it would all happen swiftly and that was something that she would have to be prepared for. All she had to do was remind him of his lust, awaken it in him, and then see just what her sweet, clumsy Gael wanted to do.

He shifted his weight above her, but she wasn't about to stop and ask if he was okay, the tight line of his abdominals and sternum hustling on her on. There was pleasure indeed to come and she could only push on, striving for it as the soft fold of his sheath loomed. It was tucked up close between his hind legs for protection with a pair of furry balls behind, but Miya could not have said that she'd really paid them all that much attention before to them, even when he was stretched out. It had taken her a while to come into herself and understand just what it meant to be a gryphon hen but that did not mean by any stretch of the imagination that she was not interested in all of the normal things that gryphon hens *were* interested in…

He chirped and she did not hesitate, boldly running her tongue out and over his nuts, cradling and stroking them as she tested their weight and virility. Aware of just what they contained, she grunted softly and nuzzled into them, cherishing the era of vitality that they rushed to herald in. And all of it would soon be ploughed deep into her needy pussy.

"So full…" She breathed as they plumped up and dropped for her, bearing witness to the crudity of her words. "I knew you'd be needy… You've never done this before either, have you, Gael?"

But the drake didn't know, still, what she meant, although his hips rocked eagerly and he nodded, beak parted as his tongue spilt out. Pant after pant dragged through his throat and down his windpipe but it didn't serve to get any more air into his lungs as he adjusted his stance and groaned deep in the back of his throat as his cock, very slowly, slipped out. And that was something that not even Miya could have ever claimed to have seen before, despite their closeness growing up, his shaft hardening into a slick spire that tapered to a smooth point.

Yet more and more grew from his sheath, boasting his size and virility and she could not help but rush into the next course of action, taking him into her beak even as she hustled along. It was clumsy and, really, she should have waited but Miya could not, every last bit of her body yearning for him and the pleasure that that lustrous breeding spire could give her. With it driving up into the back of her maw as it thickened and seemed to grow even more, she could not see it but she imagined it gleaming with pre-cum and saliva, the salty muskiness of the former drooling thickly onto her tongue as he shuffled and gasped.

What did Gael think of all that? Ah, there was no time in her mind to slow down and wait, to see what was happening, heart pounding, need rising more and more with every passing second. Her sex clenched down on nothing even though it oh so very desperately needed something, hissing around his hot length, the thickness of him stretching it to its limit. It was just supposed to be a way that a hen could get a male all hot and ready for her but there was so much more that Miya wanted from him now that she'd begun, moaning and grunting like a seasoned brood hen. Her tongue did not know quite how to move but she gave it her best shot, curling the slippery length up and around his girth, teasing down the smoothness to where there was a slight ridge framing the very head of his shaft.

And the very moment that she teased up to those glands had the gryphon tensing and huffing, grunting as he rounded his lower back as if to thrust, need taking over. He didn't need to know how to move, only to let instinct take over, sweet moment by moment. Snarling deep in the back of his throat, he hissed and rapped his beak, movements sharp and juddery as she drew back in time only to slurp and suckle oh so very desperately on the head of his cock as if there was nothing else for her. In all honesty, she could have stayed down there beneath him in the midst of breeding lust and sucked his fat shaft for eternity, or at least until exhaustion took her – but she was not in the realm of sensibility at that time.

More and more… The musk of him softened, creamier pre-cum flowing into her mouth. Was that how all drakes came to the point of orgasm? Of course, he was not quite there yet but, in her mind, he was giving her all the signs of being close, at least, not even able to talk as his beak clacked, huffing and shifting his weight, unable to stay still for even a moment. And Miya sucked harder still, trying to make her cheeks hollow out from the force of it, his slick essence pouring down her throat as she gulped and gulped and gulped. Was that his climax?

No… No, his orgasm was much, *much* stronger than that. And she didn't even have a single moment of warning before the first blast, quite literally, hit her in the back of her maw. It was fortunate that she did not possess the capability to gag or expel content from her throat as her eyes bugged out, swallowing as hard and as fast as she possibly could to keep up with the relentless stream, a creamy flow of gryphon-cum splattering her maw. Thick rivulets drooled from the corners of her beak where she was not quick enough to gulp it down but the thrust and grind of his shaft didn't make it any easier as the drake pushed and pushed, as desperate for the exotic pleasure she offered him as she was to take it down, all of it.

But she needed something more now – she was a hen! And giving a blowjob, something that they had, in fact, picked up from human talk, would not satisfy her as an invisible claw clenched in her gut, telling her that her job wasn't done yet. No, that task would not be complete until her needs were filled too, arousal flooding the air as if her body was striving, not without due cause, to saturate it entirely with her essence.

Out from under him, she blinked and swayed, licking his seed off her beak, splattered in it but happily so. She needed that taste in her mouth, the musk of him under her tongue, falling and falling deeper into the very breeding lust that she'd thought it would be so easy to tease him into. Maybe it had not been Gael, after all, that had needed to be prepared for mating when her pussy squeezed and rippled erratically as if it knew something too that she did not.

He growled, eyes fierce and a smirk glittering in them, beak parted. A hard length of gryphon-meat refused to retract into its sheath, only just getting warmed up, and she gasped, head spinning with the raw, powerful knowledge of what was to come. There could only be one outcome and every last drop of blood in her body *sang* for it.

She needed him, pure and simple.

"Gael…"

Her eyes burned as she turned her tail to him, the gryphon bowing down her front and raising her back end for him, tail lifted high to show off the swollen folds of her sex, needing him so very much more than she could ever have put into words. But that was part of the need of a gryphon hen that they could put it into their actions and the sway of her hindquarters was more than enough to draw in the lust-addled gryphon drake, Gael panting heavily as he could not help but lunge for her, driving his beak wantonly up under her tail, licking and slurping at her sex as if it was all that he needed in the world, the whole wide world. And, to a gryphon in such an acute state of breeding need, it really was. Every last inch of his body throbbed and pulsed with the need to fuck, to mate, to breed and there no longer was any question at all as to whether or not Miya would be a lucky enough hen to leave their hasty, sweetening interlude with a clutch quickening in her belly.

His tongue drove deep, spreading her open even as her breath caught, eyes rolling back and the line of her bowed spine tight with barely restrained tension.

"Take me!"

It was time and both knew it, her juices laying heavy on his beak, Miya quivering beneath him, aching for his weight on her back, bearing her down. She would take his force, however, and had no qualms about the consequences of her actions, craving everything he had to give her from those swinging, churning balls, throbbing with unrestrained need. Hissing through his beak, Gael mounted her swiftly. There never should have been any question about it, not really.

After all… Just what kind of drake would he have been to refuse?

# Rainy Day Lust

## Part Two

Bowing her forelegs down to the ground, Miya moaned and clacked the edges of her beak together urgently, needing him perhaps even more than he needed her. Her cunny twitched, almost pulling up reminiscent of another species of creature that could be just as lustful as a gryphon, beak parted to pant. Flanks heaving, the gryphon's golden-eagle type head rolled back, unable to do anything, frozen in place before the partner that she craved so terribly, her tail flagged so high that it spilt over her back in a sleekly leonine curve, the brown fur of her feline half gleaming with good health. And yet she hoped for more health than ever, stomach plumping out with a clutch of eggs that she would call her own, need coming to a beautiful head as it had always been meant to.

It was enough to draw in any male but there was only one that she wanted, one that she craved so very desperately above all else. Gael stared at her as if he'd seen a ghost, his cock still hanging below his stomach, drooling with the last throbs of orgasm. And yet she needed more so very quickly, her cunny not needing any preparation at all for that massive hunk of gryphon-flesh even though the gryphon drake in question surely needed a little more time to recover than she was willing to give him.

Grunting, he tucked his head instinctively around to preen his white feathers, eyes sharp and wide, although he could be glad for instinct taking over at the point where it mattered the most. Neither of them had had a lover before, even though Miya had spoken with the hens of the flock many times about sex and what to expect. That was not a replacement for the real thing when it came down to it.

"P-please," she begged him, for she was hardly able to force him to mount her, not unless she wanted to drastically change their positions and the like for some other feather of pleasure. "Take me! Oh, feather-lords, I need you so much!"

Gael swallowed hard. She'd never talked to him like that before but there was something very different about the lustfully seductive hen that stood before him, her chest bowed down to the ground, hips raised and tail flaunting her scent all over the place. And yet he needed a moment in which to understand what was happening, half-closing his eyes as he breathed deeply and heavily, rasping through his nares as he sucked in her delicious aroma over and over again.

"Yes… Yesss…"

It was a hiss that did not seem natural coming from her beak and, startled, Miya jerked her head back around, staring over her shoulder with wide eyes (although gryphons, typically, had wider eyes than most anyway).

"What? Gael… What are you doing?"

But the drake had savoured her scent enough and knew now what he wanted to do with her, tracing the tip of his moist tongue along the edge of his beak, relishing in the moment. Was this what it was to breed, to fuck? His cock throbbed up into ridges, pumping up thick and full with blood as if to nod to the older heritage of their kind when they had barbs to catch and pull into a partner's sex or any breeding hole, really. They were much softer than that but jutted out from his cock in an aggressive fashion, something headier and thicker again still swelling right at the base of his length.

Now had come the time to breed. Nearly.

Miya jumped as a heavy forepaw landed on her hindquarters, holding her still, but she didn't have a chance to ask what Gael was doing as his beak pressed up against her pussy, that delicious slit of feminine flesh that begged him in so. Although his cock was still hard, he needed time to recover himself and he would take that by bringing a fresh rise to her, cunny twitching and clenching even as his tongue, very delicately, spread her open.

The moan that rose from Miya's lips ruffled his feathers up in all the right ways. Yes, that was what he needed, what the tightening in his gut was driving him on and on to claim for his own. He could not have said just why it had come up inside him that day of all days as the storm snarled outside the bounds of the cave, rain streaming down in a sheet that allowed none to penetration, yet she was there before him. Something had shifted between them and he would have been less of a drake not to rise to the call of it with a shrill keen, pressing his beak up and into her sex to savour of her essence.

And she was sweet, so very sweet. He jerked back, startled by the taste, and licked his beak without thinking, scooping more and more of her sweet flavour into his beak. Miya quivered and shuddered, mumbling something, but Gael was lost to her charm, wanting more of what lay in her honey pot. Again, the smooth curve of his beak teased up to her sex and she groaned, huffing against the floor, tail winding around his neck as if that would be enough to keep him there. In all honesty, neither one of them was going to move away in a hurry but the hormones flooding them from the inside out snarled and snapped, striving to tell them to get a move on, to come together before it was too late and one of them grew tired of the fuss.

Gryphons were a fickle sort indeed!

Miya moaned and rubbed her beak on the ground, head swimming and pulsating on wave after wave of pleasure. Every muscle in her body screamed that she was right where she needed to be, head down and submissive, eyes half-lidded. What did she need to see for, after all? There was nothing for her but sensation as his tongue dug lightly into her, seeming to be acting on an impulse to seek out a part of her that not even her claws had touched, although she had also heard the older gryphon hens talking about that. That pleasure, however, was a sort best gleaned from a willing partner.

She knew the very moment that he'd found it too, head shooting up and a low chuff bursting from her beak, mouth hanging open lewdly as if she'd all of a sudden lost control of the muscles there. That sensitive patch of nerves that came together in the right place, more sensitive than a male's dick – or so she was told. It didn't matter in the lust of the moment as she squealed and ground back on him, tongue pushing out lustfully over the edge of her beak as she clacked the edges together for him, begging for more, wanting so very much more.

"Ohhh!"

Orgasm was not a foreign concept to her, although it was not something that she had ever before had for herself, his tongue slurping crudely up inside her without any measure of skill or finesse. But Gael didn't need to have experience to please her and he licked and licked, letting her moan and grind back on him, the curve of the upper side of his beak teasing into her softness, daring to push ever so slightly into her folds. Of course, she controlled how far back she thrust – at least, in part. Miya, after the fact, would say that she was not in control of anything at all at that moment, prey to instinct and breeding lust. All she wanted was to be fucked, to have that long, thick rod of gryphon-meat slammed into her over and over again, the ridges and light undulations catching as she was made well and truly into a brood hen.

The barbs too, oh... She'd run her tongue around those and they'd been divine even then, the hen craving him, the something more that he could offer her, all the raw power in the stud drake. Miya had never before known or understood that he had in him. Of course, she'd had to bring that side out of her friend, but he keened and crooned eagerly into her vent as he slurped away, digging his tongue in and deeper, searching for that final barrier within her that sealed off her womb.

Gael's eyes half-closed, breathing in short, sharp puffs of breath. Was this what it was to breed, to be a breeder? To be strong, to be powerful... To let his cock slap up against his belly as he ached to breed her? And yet he knew in the back of his mind, however dim the thought was, that Miya deserved her pleasure and her fun too, needing more from him even though the slickness of her cunny denoted that she very clearly did not need any manner of preparation. Maybe she was just that deep into her season...

It didn't matter. All that mattered was that he kept curling and winding his tongue, scooping out mouthful after mouthful of that sweet nectar, tasting deeply of her. His balls ached for release and he bid his body to be still, to be quiet, to have patience while he worked himself up again. He could have fucked her right there and then, but it would have lost something, the friend that he had known for so many years turning into something all the more delectable in the blink of an eye.

He needed her and he suckled her juices wantonly into his mouth and his beak, tongue curling and flicking, her sweet juices flicking everywhere. But Gael wasn't even aware of the mess he was in the process of making as he lapped and lapped, eyes half-lidded and a low croon rising from his throat. He was merely a beast of passion in the midst of lovemaking, adoring all that was laid before him, cock hard and pulsing, wanting more, so much more, than his befuddled brain so far had the sense and presence of mind to take.

Miya's breath ramped up, although it didn't feel as if she was getting very much oxygen into her lungs at all. The hen's head rolled and she strove to contain herself, trembling as her front legs buckled, crushing her chest lightly down to the floor as if she could not simply contain the weight of her body anymore, or even think of supporting it. She needed it, needed it so badly, hips working and humping and grinding mindlessly. Why wouldn't he give it to her?

The drake rumbled a sexy growl against her folds, those tremors rising through her, a tantalising seduction that had to grab her, draw her in against all the odds. Maybe it was wrong that they had come together after so much time of being friends, but it felt right to, such a familiar beak pressing into her, spreading her folds and her vent apart. He dug into her as if he had a right to be there and she hissed anxiously, grinding on the edges of her beak, that cord of tightness drawing tauter and tauter within her. There was no holding back and he, Gael, would be the one to truly unleash the storm within her, flapping and bucking maniacally as she, once again, lost control of her body and her mind with the only other gryphon in the world that really and truly mattered to her.

He pushed on, slurping and suckling the best he could with a beak, lacking lips, but it was more than enough for a lusty gryphon hen like her and Miya keened out shrilly as orgasm crashed over her, feathers ruffled and dropping to the ground as if she was shedding in a time of stress. But she was far, far from stressed in the heat of the moment, wanting more and more, always more, pleasure throbbing and pulsating through her as if it was controlled to the beat of music performed around a raging fire pit at the height of a gryphon ceremony. And it was a ceremony of sorts too to be bequeathed such an orgasm in the prelude to her breeding, her deflowering, all that she'd ever wanted and more.

Gael licked his beak, lapping her vent over and over again, the tip of his tongue circling her clit. But he didn't stop, couldn't stop, suckling down every last drop of her orgasm that he could get into his ever-hungry maw. The gryphoness thrust back and flipped up her tail but there was nothing at all that could have stopped her orgasm from crashing on, rising and falling like a tide that kept on coming, breaking the flood barriers and sweeping through, laying waste to towns. It was powerful, it was raw – it was everything that she just was not able to take for herself on her own.

Panting, she dipped her beak, laying her chin on the cave floor, storm raging on. Forked lightning sliced through the sky, a reminder of the force of nature that could take them at any time, and her gryphon mate pushed over her back at the very moment that a roll of thunder clamoured through. The grinding roar snarled as Gael fumbled for purchase, driven entirely by breeding instinct as the rampant, hard tip of his cock brushed her folds.

Time seemed to slow, the pouring rain nowhere near enough to cover up their harsh, ragged breaths raking through lungs over and over again, clawing at their innards. They were nothing more than gryphons right there and then, snarling and growling, words failing them when they may well have wanted them. They just needed to be together, to feel their bodies joining, but Gael had not the finesse to drive into her straight off the bat, his tail lashing furiously as he tried to sink home over and over again.

Alas, that was the problem with orgasm – it made everything just too slippery to deal with! Gael snapped and ground the edges of his beak together, intent on pushing into her, the ridges on his cock plumping up even thicker and fuller, the bulge at the base of his shaft already engorged too. It was there to pull their bodies together at the height of orgasm, ensuring that every last drop of seed pumped into her, but it wasn't meant to be so large so soon, making everything all the more difficult once he was inside.

The tip of his cock had to catch in the right hole sooner or later, however, and the two of them trilled out pleasantly in turn as he sank in, inch after inch ploughing into her. He wriggled his hindquarters and pushed in deeper and deeper, finding some kind of thrust in himself, the grind wedging his cock in. Miya panted but every sound she made was a croon for more that readily leapt to her beak, pushing on and on, getting every last bit of cock into her that she deserved.

No more could Miya claim that she was a virgin, hormones ramped up, the air thick with the scent of sex and musk and the fresh fall of rain just beyond the mouth of the cave itself. Her cherry was well and truly popped, her passage stretching wonderfully around that deliciously thick hunk of gryphon-meat. And, still, she needed more, feeling as if she was being stretched to her breaking point, although everything was well within her capabilities and she had to trust in that too. With her chest pinned down, she was utterly and beautifully helplessly submissive before him, her tail wound around his neck as she moaned out his name over and over again.

*Gael, Gael, Gael...*

He would always be the one for her and it was funny just how a male's cock could change that in her, make her feel that at the crux of the moment.

Everything came together at just the right time, his balls slapping up against her pussy, the gryphon drake as deep as he could possibly go. He keened shrilly, the tip of his cock wedged up alongside her innermost barrier, pushing into the soft part of the flesh there so it was not uncomfortable, although that was only a happy accident on his part rather than any measure of skill.

But Miya screeched for more, clawing at the floor and arching back, her tail flicking, the hair at the tip lashing back and forth, over and over again. There was no rhyme or reason to the thrusting gyrations of her body, every last fibre of her being snarling for more, craving it, heaving for it – all she knew was that she *needed* it! And he was willing to deliver it all to her in spades, slamming in, his working to use every last inch of his cock, the tip drooling and drooling, the flow of pre-cum seemingly unable to stop. He heaved for breath but never quite seemed to get enough of it into his lungs but that he would be able to breathe freely again was debatable until the deed was good and done.

And he had to keep going, had to keep thrusting, beak dipping sensually to her neck to lick and nibble tenderly at the back of her feathered nape. Gael still had some presence of mind even then and pressed in closer, his hindquarters scooting in and down, ensuring that he had the best possible angle to thrust from, learning more and more with a very steep learning curve. Each thrust came with a little more ease and finesse than the last and he let the hump and grind of her body guide him, Miya whimpering and keening. Even then, her moans told him when he had hit just the right spot and he did the best he could to hit that same spot repeatedly, driving over the most sensitive parts of her passage as the ridges caught and massaged her so very deliciously inside.

She couldn't stop herself, rising closer and closer to that threshold of orgasm as he pounded her there, the not-so-much-a-virgin squealing and cawing, wings spread and trembling in sweet submission. It was right, so very right, to be down there on the ground beneath him, panting and gasping, her eyes barely open. All she needed was the wash of sensation crashing over her, each driving slam of his shaft making her want to orgasm all over again, beak opening and closing even though she could not honestly be sure whether there was sound coming from her beak or not. It didn't matter, nothing else mattered, as long as he just kept fucking her, growling into her ear and even nibbling lightly along the tufts that denoted just where the light indents of her ears were.

Her pussy clenched and sucked around his cock as if her body was loathe to let him go, holding him tight as he snarled and tried to go harder, always harder. Gael snapped and pounded her like he'd never done before and that was too much for Miya, screeching and clawing at the stone floor as lightning split the sky and she climaxed on his achingly hard shaft. If it was even possible, his lusty shaft plumped up further inside her, the ridges thickening and stiffening, that delightful bulge at the base pressing ever more insistently against the edges of her pussy, her vent spreading and stretching, wanting so very desperately to accept him.

Gael gasped, throat tense, even the mere act of swallowing beyond him. Her cunny rippling around him, milking him... It was too much for a no longer virgin drake to bare, snarling and slamming, hind legs scrabbling to get further under him, to give him more purchase as he thrust and thrust, looking for that ultimate completion. Her juices soaked his shaft as they had his tongue and he couldn't stop, wouldn't stop, his thrusts ramping up as he forced the bulge there into her too, her passage welcoming him even as she keened, a trembling mess of fur and feathers beneath him, far from the hen that he had once known.

No, she was better than that. She was his *mate*.

And so it would be until the end of their days together as his balls tightened, swinging and churning, the drake able to finally able to recognise what it meant to have an orgasm rising up, demanding attention. He could not ignore it either as he drove in, on the edge, his short, shallow thrusts leaving his cock as deep inside her as it was possible to be as Miya's orgasm rolled on and on, thrumming up inside her like a song that would never truly reach completion.

Maybe that's just how the relationship between them would be?

The first jet of cum shooting into her caught her by surprise and Miya jerked, Gael taking a tighter grip on her still, cock spurting madly. Hot, so very hot... She didn't think she should truly have been so sensitive as to be able to feel each and every last jet of his cum splashing inside her, but she did, the sloshing spill of cum flooding her womb, forced up in there even through the tight barrier of her cervix, the volume simply too much for her body to otherwise hold. And yet it could not drool out around the length of his cock either as that bulge sealed them lusciously together, stretching her wider than ever, every last drop left inside her as he rested over her back, trusting her to bear his weight even as her legs trembled shockingly.

*So, this is what it is to be bred...*

The hen smiled faintly, her beak parted and eyes half-lidded, soaring her way gently back to the world of the waking as he pumped her full, her stomach swelling more and more, a pleasant bulge forming around her flanks as her belly was forced to take it. Of course, it was really her womb filling up with his seed, but her body showed it as if she was heavy with a clutch of eggs already and she imagined it to be such as that creamy seed pooled within her, seeding her eggs while she crooned breathlessly and tried to turn her beak tiredly back against his.

And he was right there, clucking and crooning to her as she moaned, two bodies joined in the heat of lust, relaxing together, the afterglow coming upon them softly and sweetly. There was no rush, not with the storm easing off ever so slightly outside, the fall of rain lessening – yet it was still more than enough to keep the outside world away from them, leaving them to be with one another and only one another while the rest of the world waited out the weather too.

"Stay with me."

Gael nuzzled the back of her neck tenderly.

"Always."

*

Months later, a very fat gryphoness waddled to the front of the cave into which she'd settled into with Gael to raise their flock, although she was still yet to lay her clutch of eggs. Smiling at the light of dawn, she crooned to the now fully developed eggs in her stomach, sitting back on her haunches as the round fullness of her stomach begged her for a break. The eggs shifted against one another constantly, tiny muscular contractions that happened without her mind or consent ensuring that they were rotated in the incubator of her womb, safe and sound until the time came for their laying.

Yet that seemed to be earlier than she'd expected as a strange pulse echoed through her, shivering and hackles raising as if something had startled her. Eyeing the landscape before her, the valley stretching out safe and sound in the golden touch of dawn, she saw nothing amiss and made as if to shrug it off until another clench rose through her, demanding attention this time.

*Oh…*

She'd never thought it would feel quite like that.

"Gael…"

Of course, he was right there behind her and rushed to her side, crooning and pressing up against her, comforting her with the warm length of his body as he pressed in, eyes alit and intent.

"Is it time?"

Another contraction rippled through her, although this one came with a deep sense of satisfaction unlike any other. Yet all was new to a gryphoness bearing her first clutch and she could only be thankful that she had Gael there to hold her sweetly, loving her and giving her the support she needed through the laying.

Smiling faintly with gentle eyes, beak parted, she nudged his cheek, tail intertwined with his.

"Everything's going to change now, isn't it?"

And it most certainly was. But they would, as they always had, do it all together.

The time had come.

# Fertility

Eden moaned, the feline anthro's toes curling as she lay back on the bed, her fox partner kissing reverently over her stomach. Nude but for her bare, white fur, the cat shuddered under him, her heart beating more quickly than it ever had before.

Well, that was perhaps an over exaggeration. It could not be anything less than that even as she whimpered and moaned, Charlie sliding between her thighs as he parted them readily.

"I can't wait to see your pregnant belly," he murmured huskily, the red fox nuzzling her inner thighs, taking his time with her. "You're going to be such a good mom."

Ah, for where was the true fun to be had in breeding without thinking of all that was to come after, hm? They knew that, it was not about the fantasy. It was about what it meant for them, their lives together, how everything was going to change…

And it was about that moment too, adoring her, Charlie kissing her stomach, shivering as he imagined it rising with their offspring in the months to come. Of course, neither the cat nor the fox knew how long it would take them to conceive, but they would find out what was to come for them, all in good time.

The feline rolled her hips up as her lover's muzzle dipped back between her thighs, lapping slowly and softly at her pussy. His tongue caressed her pussy so very sweetly, just about prying open her folds, dipping between them and dragging tentatively up against her clit. It was not that Charlie didn't know what to do, of course, but he wanted to take his time, licking and kissing, testing her reactions.

"Ah, oh, please…" She breathed, an arm flung back across the pillow, her long, blue hair a halo around her head. "Please, I need you inside me… You tease me so much, Charlie… I love it, but… Oh!"

She bucked her hips up again, head spinning with need, though she ached for more, so much more. Yet it was her lovely fox who made sure she wouldn't rush over the edge into it, savouring the sweetness of the moment and offering it up to Eden to see if she would like to relish in it too.

Not everything, after all, had to be rushed through with haste, almost forgetting to relax and enjoy along the way. So, he slowed things down for her, slipping his tongue inside her pussy and curling it up inside her, seeking her G-spot. It was not the easiest cluster of overly sensitive nerve endings for him to seek, but his tongue twitched over the spot curiously, sensing the very faint difference in the texture of her sweet, velvety passage. Charlie had not spent enough time with other partners to tell whether or not that was normal, but it was true for her.

And it gave him something of a guide as he moaned into her sex and kissed her pussy deeply, the feline twisting lightly and bucking her hips, though she didn't grind up too hard against Charlie. Oh, how her fox mesmerised her. He was wonderful, so sweet, so very kind, always thinking of her first and foremost. One day, she really hoped she could treat the wonderful fox even half as well as he treated her.

The fox would have, of course, thought she treated him even better than he treated her – but that was just one of the little reasons their relationship worked as well as it did.

"Mmmph... Oh... Please..."

"Mm, you have to be patient, sweetheart," Charlie chuckled, drawing back from her pussy only enough to talk, lapping off her sweetly tart arousal from the side of his muzzle. "This time... It's just for us. For us, right now."

"I know, I know..."

Eden stretched and curled her toes, flexing them as she extended her body to its greatest extent, her arms up over her head. Her fox always brought her back down to earth and yet her skin prickled and tingled with exotic affliction, aching for him desperately, the light burning and simmering sensation flowing through her deviously.

Charlie grinned subtly as he kissed his way up her body again, nuzzling her stomach once more and spending some time there, though there was no real rush, none at all. But he wanted to take his time adoring her breasts and kissing them, nuzzling softly into the gentle flesh and leaving a brief, light indent from his nose in its wake whenever he withdrew.

"Mmm… Your breasts too…" He breathed. "It's not all about this…but…"

Eden giggled, stroking his head and ruffling the thicker patch of rich, russet fur he had between his ears.

"I know… But you like my breasts. I wonder how big they're going to get?"

"It's not about that," he grumbled, kissing her nipples and even catching one between his lips to pull them out softly from her chest. "You're going to *glow* and everything else is going to look… I can't imagine you being even better than you are, but…"

"Oh, you think you're so clever with words, don't you?"

The feline giggled flirtatiously and surprised the fox by rolling him over before he could get to her lips and seduce her with a kiss. Rolling him on to his back by hooking her hind paw around his ankle, she sat astride him briefly, her tail lashing back and forth. Only then did Eden crawl, slowly but surely, up the length of his body to seat herself at the top of his chest, as if she was going to sit on his muzzle. Not that it would have been a bad thing at all for the cat to do, just a little unexpected for her.

"Mmm… Imagine how my stomach is going to look," she purred, her tail still sweeping back and forth across his stomach, teasing him lightly as it caught the rise of his cock. "You're going to be looking up at me like this, when you're eating me out, and there's going to be this big, smooth rise… Our little one growing inside me."

"Mmmph, oh, Eden…" Charlie groaned, his fingers digging lightly into her thighs, though the fox was careful of his short claws. "You really know how to get to me… In a good way."

"Well, I'd be disappointed if it was any other way, hon," she teased, wriggling on top of him. "But I think there's a part of you that needs attention too, even though I know you just want to be inside me already, breeding me…"

The fox moaned. Oh, yes… Yes, he very much wanted to be inside her, his muzzle bowed down reverently to her breasts, kissing and nipping, suckling on her nipples just to give her a little more pleasure. Yet she slid back from him, not easing into the position Charlie had in his mind, but taking everything into her own paws, as she always did. He would have expected nothing else from the canny feline as her tail flicked and curled back and forth, seating herself across his hips.

His shaft jutted up before her and, of course, Eden openly lied about him needing to be ready for her. It was all part of her play as she folded her fingers sensually around the throbbing length of his cock and Charlie swallowed a moan, not wanting to sound too needy about everything, not even in a moment like that.

He wanted her, ached for her more than anything, but he paced himself, grunting as she wrapped her hand around his cock, pumping the hard length very slowly up and down. She squeezed at the base, where his fox-ish knot would form when he was ready for it, though Charlie didn't know how long he was going to hold back with her.

Not when his fertile goddess was on top of him, rising to present the very tip of his cock to the soft, sweet folds of her pussy. Her tail swept over his legs and Eden breathed out evenly, her thick eyelashes fluttering.

He could almost imagine how wonderful, more wonderful than usual, she was going to look when she was pregnant, taking everything in paw. The feline sank on to his cock and, in his mind's eye, the fox saw her pregnant, her hair longer and thicker, gleaming with a lustrous sheen. Her belly rose before him, the additional weight of her body simply exquisite, though he'd already started working out a little harder to make sure he could still carry her when she was pregnant. He didn't want her to have to lift a finger that she didn't want to, taking care of her every need.

So fertile, so beautiful... He was sure it wouldn't take them long at all to conceive and his heart pounded as, for the first time in years, his shaft sank into her, bare. Of course, the feline had gone off her contraceptive pill too, so there was nothing restraining them from conceiving, nothing at all.

"Oh, Eden..."

He moaned, rolling his hips up, though he didn't dictate the moment, allowing Eden that control. His fertility goddess more than deserved it, every moment of it, he was sure, though he let his jaws hang open for a rather plaintive whine as he twisted his head back, trying to hold on. Charlie's knot threatened to plump up and swell right there and then, though the fox did his best to hold it back. It would not be the only round with

Eden that night, he was sure, the light dimming beyond the window and the crack in the curtains.

"Mmmm… Relax, Charlie," she purred, her voice low and throaty. "You tell me to take things slower, don't you? Well, this is the moment right now… You're going to let me ride you, nice and slow…"

She paused, her eyes glowing with a devious feline intensity.

"And then…" She murmured, her voice dropping to a huskier tone. "You're going to do everything you want to me, my stud of a fox. Do you like the sound of that?"

"Mmm… Oh!" Charlie gasped, breathless as she bucked, rising and falling more sharply on his cock than he had anticipated, startling him. "Yes… Oh… Anything you want… Eden…"

Yet he was along for the ride well and truly that time as Eden took control, his thickness filling her just right, though she yearned to grind down on to his hard knot too. That would come in time, she was sure about that, but maybe the fox had something in mind for her.

She couldn't wait to see, taking her cues from his grunts and groans, rising and falling more slowly on his cock than that first hump of her hips. That had just been to catch the vulpine off-guard, something she didn't all that often manage, though all was right with the world, as long as they were together. Neither one of them was more dominant or submissive, not really, in the bedroom, but they enjoyed passing the leading role back and forth between them, just to see what the other would come up with.

"Mmmm… Ohhh…"

Her sweet fox groaned under her and she smirked faintly, splaying out her paw on his chest, her fingers extended. She had very small claws, though they were more like the nails she had seen on some anthros, though everyone was different in how their bodies were put together with those little nuances.

*Imagine how tiny our little one's claws will be,* Eden thought, the notion leaping unbidden into her mind. *So small, so delicate.*

A warm, maternal urge surged in her and she let out a breathless yowl as she rode her partner, the pace of her hips speeding up, just a little. Yet she didn't want him to get off so quickly, no, not when she could draw things out for longer, enjoying his adoring gaze on her, his eyes shining as if she was the only thing in the world.

Earlier in their relationship, she'd found that embarrassing, though sweet, to be looked at like that. Now, she understood why Charlie was so open about his affection with her, for she felt exactly the same way about him.

"Mmm... You feel so good inside me..." She moaned, shuddering on top of him as the tremor sent her tail fluffing up, ever so slightly. "And your knot... Mmm... It's going to stretch me out so nicely."

Eden leaned forward, purring, her throat and chest trembling with the soft, subtle sound. Charlie grunted, eyes on her, never once leaving Eden in some way.

"And you're going to pin me," she breathed. "Breed me, fuck me. Show me how virile you are... While we see just how fertile I am."

He barked a short laugh, though it was of surprise more than amusement, his shaft throbbing deliciously inside the wet heat of her pussy.

"Oh, Eden... I didn't think you'd come out with something like that," the fox confessed, his tail trying to wag where it was trapped under his rump. "I'd keep you in the bedroom all week if I could, even taking you in the shower when we went...mm...to freshen up. Just breeding and filling you over and over again until my balls are sore and I have nothing left to give."

"Oh, I think you'll always have something to give me, darling," she moaned, trembling on top of him. "I know you will…"

He swept his paws up her sides, caressing her breasts and giving them a soft squeeze, but Charlie's fingers were really up there so he could tease her nipples, trapping them between his fingers. The gentle squeeze had her arching up into his touch, her chest pressing forward, and the cat moaned, hair mussed up and yet she was more beautiful than ever before him.

"Mmm, I'm going to take such good care of you, darling," he moaned, barely with himself in the moment, awash in sensation. "I'm going to fill you so many times… So many times that there's no way you're leaving tonight without a bun in the oven."

It was so easy to get swept up in fantasies, yet it was those very fantasies, playing out in reality, that turned them on, skin flushed under their fur as the bed squeaked beneath them. Eden couldn't help increasing the pace of her hips, grinding down on to his cock, even though she had drawn it all out for longer than even she had thought she'd be able to already.

Some things, like his throbbing hard-on inside her, just felt too good for her to resist. Especially as that cord of desire tautened within, threatening to snap. Yet it was a good kind of snapping, the kind that brought with it a release, and she toyed with that cord, the edge of ecstasy shivering through her body.

"Mmm… So close…"

Charlie could have taken over, but he let her sink into him as he whined, his knot finally swelling fully from where it had grown chunky and chubby: a little more challenging for her to take, but not impossible. Once it was inside, however, she ground deep and squeezed, encouraging him to swell fully inside her, the tapered head of his shaft questing for her innermost barrier, even though he could not quite reach it. He didn't need to, not when that would have been uncomfortable for her, and she moaned out his name as she waited, his paw creeping down between their bodies.

The moment his fingers caught and rubbed her clit was too much for her, bringing her over the edge as overstimulation sent the feline tumbling into the freefall of orgasm. Her pussy clenched, squeezing his shaft, yet the pull of her muscles contracting around him was erratic and entirely out of Eden's control. There was no way for the cat to know how hard she was going to squeeze, not as the fox's maw hung open and he howled, knot pulsating inside her, his balls surely ready to spill.

And spill he did, though Charlie would have held out longer if he could have done so, all to bear witness to his fertility goddess of a lover on top of him, her strong, thick thighs wrapped around him while she straddled his hips. His paw rested over her crotch, the other up on her stomach, fingers slick with her arousal while he rubbed her clit, though his ministrations were rather clumsy and sloppy, torn with the pulse of his own ecstasy.

Ropes of thick, creamy seed flooded her pussy, pulse after pulse, and, to the fox, it felt like he was cumming harder than ever before, his shaft spilling more and more seed inside her, losing himself in the moment. Yet there was nowhere else the fox or the cat needed to be other than in one another's arms, relaxing there and riding out the high of orgasm, together.

She eased down before he did, slumping towards him, the fox just about getting his arms up in time to catch Eden in them. She laid her head on his chest, nuzzling up higher into the crook of his neck, purring all the while. Yet the fox was not done yet, groaning faintly as his cock continued spending his load inside her, marvelling vaguely at the force of his own climax.

*It's been a long time since I go off like that…*

*It's just what Eden does to me.*

She would always be special to him, but maybe it was due to how Charlie held the feline in such high regard that he always had more pleasure with her, every time. His arms went around her, the pressure of his knot tugging at her pussy, but Eden didn't seem to mind, her purrs only intensifying as she relaxed in the afterglow of their first breeding of the night.

For there was much more to come, wanting to see her fertility put to the test, though that side of things was for their own fun. Whether it took one night, a few weeks or several months was by-the-by for them, as long as they had one another.

In the love of one another and breeding lust, the fox and the feline could finally see just where the next step in their lives was ready to take them.

Together.

Always together.

# Sabre-Toothed Lust

Selsei growled, scenting the air. The sabre-toothed cat hunkered down low to the ground, his fur a golden orange, richly shaded, though that was difficult to see in the dead of the night. Colours did not come out as easily then, though he painted a picture of the world around him in another way, the shades of grey of the rough and rugged land, more mountainous and craggier than where Selsei had been born, as vibrant as they were in the day.

Sabre-toothed felines, after all, did not hunt very often by day. Their bodies were lean and yet muscular, not a spare ounce of fat held on their feral, four-legged bodies, though they were blocky and strong. They were built for short bursts of speed over stamina and hunting and dragging down bigger prey was not something that they could do when they did not either have the element of surprise or, of course, the ability of the pack to corner them.

His long teeth curved out, betraying his size and strength, eyes gleaming in the darkness as his chops slavered and drooled. Scenting the air, the feline chuffed softly, digging his claws into the dirt, feeling how it shifted under him, leaving an imprint of all that had gone before. Yet there was nothing that could overrule the scent on the breeze, licking at his nostrils, feeding into his system that had Selsei's loins stirring.

The sabre-toothed cat's tail was short, yet it could still twitch back and forth, signalling something, even when there was no one else there to see it. Oh, he knew that scent so very intimately…

"Yesss…"

Oh, his mate… Selsei's mate was out there, distracting him from the hunt, but he would go to her either way, for there was nothing in him that would resist the call of Akina. She was gorgeous, her smooth, grey coat of fur showing her muscle, her lither form, though she was larger than him, her teeth smaller. Sabre-toothed cats, after all, didn't follow the typicalness of the male being larger, for the hierarchy was tied to hunting prowess, their virility or fertility following suit.

If a male was larger, perhaps they would prove to be more dominant, higher up in the pack hierarchy. Maybe it was not in their nature. Yet there was nothing to stop a female sabre-toothed cat from taking charge, a sensual glint in her eye and a snarl tugging seductively at her lips.

His legs were in motion before his mind caught up to the passion of his body, covering the distance, though he could not keep up the stamina for all that long. It was fine, however, for Akina was not all that far away, his beauty and strong, loving female, the feline begging his attention in so many ways, even though she was not yet in his line of sight. Rocky crags towered to his right and yet he kept straight on, following her scent trail with avid exclusion of the rest of the world, trusting his status as a predator in the land to keep him safe.

Selsei's instincts took over, hind legs bunching, curling, sinking back onto them for the ultimate leap, flinging himself into the air. His eyes had not even locked onto her yet, but some part of his body, despite all that, knew that Akina was there, that all he had to do was to trust himself and all would be well. The feline yowled, breaking the air with a savage cry, yet she was right there before him, exactly as he'd predicted, as he hurled himself down from the rocks, crashing bodily into her, their forms tangling.

"Oof!"

The female sabre-toothed tiger tumbled over and over, though she had been readier for him than could have been expected of her, teeth gnashing, the scent of her heat filling the air. She growled and hurled herself right back at him, unwilling to give a single inch of ground, their claws even sinking in and touching skin in red lines of welling up blood in their rampant lust.

It was all part of what could be called a mating dance, however, between them, Selsei hissing, swiping, claws out, eyes intent. But her legs were weak from being in heat, her body running rampant with the desire for a mate who would breed her, cover her body with his until there was no longer any reason for her to get up anymore. She whimpered throatily, butting her head against his, Selsei blinking as, all of a sudden, the sabre-toothed cat realised that he was on top, pinning her down by the shoulders while her hind legs curled up against him.

"I thought you'd never come, Selsei…"

She purred cheekily, though rolling over in the clasp of his paws and claws was not something that could be done in that moment.

"Any male would follow your scent, Akina…" He growled, though there was a tease in his tone, tongue lashing out against her muzzle as he lapped, grooming her, soothing a line of blood from her nose. "Akina… My queen…"

For she was all that and more, the sabre-toothed tigers having lived together for so long that they knew each other inside and out, bodies rocking together, lust rising. Neither would have wanted to resist the influence of their heat, mating season upon them, after having three litters of cubs together already, his balls aching, though they were hidden in a thick fluff of fur in front of the join of his hind legs to his body.

His queen, Akina, knew just where to find them, however, the female tiger sliding out from under him before he could even blink, though it was all as Selsei wanted it to be. She nuzzled under his body, seeking out the slit of his sheath with her soft yet raspy tongue, needing to be gentler with her lover than she would have been with a haunch of meat. Her lover, after all, did not need the flesh stripped from him. On the contrary, all the sabre-tooth wanted to do was to coax his musky maleness out.

"Ooohhh… Akina."

He growled, though the demand in the utterance fell on deaf ears. Akina would have him one way or another even as he snarled, ducking his head, straining to contain the sharp rise in pleasure as his cock slid out. A hot length of fleshy pink, it throbbed wantonly, ridged with barbs that she had to play her tongue around very carefully. Of course, it was those very barbs that would make mating rough and carnal, something designed by his body to stimulate ovulation, though they could both be grateful that, for their species, they were not as aggressive as others. If he had tried to mate with someone who was not a sabre-toothed tiger, however, things could have been very different.

Yet Selsei had only ever been with Akina and had no intention of being with anyone else at all, not as his hind end rounded down, head spinning with lust. Oh, how she played her tongue around his cock so perfectly… It was more than enough to make his head and heart pound in the best of ways, hissing and snarling, the moon shining down, though it was the sparkling light of the stars that truly bore witness to their so very lustful tryst. It was for them, as her tongue played around the head of his cock, the male cat chuffing softly, humping and grinding, body already wanting to thrust.

"Mmmph… Deeper, Akina."

She took him into her mouth in an element of trust, tongue swirling around, pressing up to the underside, his thrusts taking him nearly all the way up into the back of her mouth. A sabre-toothed cat's muzzle was never designed for sucking cock, but they could toy with such things, their intelligence allowing them to play, experiencing more than any dumb animals that did not have their level of awareness.

That didn't stop him, however, from falling prey to instinct, thrusting and humping, trying to cling onto her with his forepaws while he chuffed and growled. Akina's chin was almost pressed all the way down to the ground as pebbles and roughed-up earth shifted under them, straining to contain it all. She growled warningly around him, but he only thrust harder, pounding against her tongue, forgetting even the need to be safe as his cock bumped up against the inside smoothness of her fangs. They could have all the trust in the world between them, but if he lost control it wouldn't matter at all.

That left it up to Akina, his mate, to take control, drawing back, not allowing him to trap her there. She had to make sure that both of them enjoyed, that they had everything they needed, even if it could be too much for them, instinct raging rampant, threatening to storm over both of them.

"Ah, easy there, darling…"

But he needed her and followed her as she slipped back, paws on her chest, forcing her over onto her back in the blink of an eye. Yet Selsei's attention was not on her muzzle or throat or even her chest, but lower down again, nuzzling, nipping, hissing through his teeth as air rasped and eased around his fangs. Her sex beckoned him, a neat slit that was ever so slightly plush and swollen with heat, tucked up under her tail hole.

"Ohhhh!"

The female tiger's cries rose to the heavens above as she cried out her delight, wriggling, his tongue delving inside. Selsei could have been gentler with her, but it was a moment in which control drifted away, letting her squirm and cry and yowl to the heavens above, the glow of the moon and stars lighting their way.

His tongue swept and dug into her, teasing her slit, feeling out the intricate softness of her velvety heat. So warm, wet, intoxicating at best... He could not help himself, forcing himself on, slurping deeply up into her, though there was no real breeding need to prepare a mate in such a way. That all came from the love between them, something that was not otherwise shown in a pack environment, secretive creatures that, even with their pack mentality and lifestyle, tended to keep themselves to themselves. It was the way of it, love coursing through, driving Selsei to taste her over and over again, pushing his tongue up as deeply inside her as he could possibly get it, all to taste every last drop of her essence.

He moaned into her, though was not lost in the moment, his cock hard and throbbing, drooling pre-cum, the thin string of it dripping to the rough ground under them. It was not the spot for lovemaking and yet where else in their territory would sabre-toothed tigers take it for their own? The ache was like nothing Selsei had felt before, cock aching more fiercely than ever, regardless of how many times they had mated before. Every time felt like the first time all over again – only more carnal and heated, more passionate than the time when they had not, truly, known what instinct was taking over their bodies.

Yet he could barely control himself, shuddering bodily, as she squirmed under him, begging him on with the shift of weight in her body alone. Her pussy drooled with her excitement for him and there was no going back from that moment, his barbs standing up a little more from his cock as his member flushed with blood, though their bodies would come together soon, one way or another.

Selsei trembled with pride as his mate, however, screamed her lust to the stars, orgasm ripping through her. He could not feel her tighten around him with his tongue sweeping in and out of her so passionately, though he could pull and tug it against her sensitive spots, everything that he had learned over their years together, drawing out her pleasure for as long as possible. Her flanks heaved and shuddered with delight, yet she had to drag in all the breath that she possibly could, even as her mate moved over her, lapping her juices off his muzzle.

"Ah… Selsei…"

Yet Akina was not his queen for no reason as she growled, lunging, working through her heat to slam into him playfully, rolling her partner onto his back. Her body lined up and she sank onto his shaft, hind legs spreading to either side of his hips, her strong, stout body finding his cock while her sex spread around him. It was a moment of perfect timing that could not possibly be replicated, though they would both reminisce about it on a more romantic night as their feral cries rose, filling the expanse of their territory while he tried to scrabble and thrust up into her.

No words were needed as they came together, male and female joined at their sexes, his barbs raking through her hot pussy while she lifted her hips for him. Yet even that scrape and jolt of pain blended into pleasure for Akina, drawing on the knowledge of experience, their bodies, hissing and snarling, twisting her head back and forth. She so very desperately needed it and he knew it too, clinging to her with his forepaws, jaws and giant sabre-teeth bared in a feral display of lust.

They would terrify all other night creatures in their territory, sending them scuttling back to their burrows and cowering in the treetops further down, though they had no interest in truly hunting that night. Their bodies called their attention far more than that, her hot sex closing around him as he raked his claws against her for leverage, neither caring about any flashes of pain or discomfort. It was all worth it for their passion and the end goal of mating, breeding, seeing her body once again swell with the bliss of new life.

There was nothing like it, snarling and hissing, rocking together, their mating position unconventional and yet one, at the same time, that worked for them. They had to make it work, for there was no way they would change positions at such a point of lust, heat coursing through, though they could only sweat through the pads of their paws. Their paws left damp prints wherever they landed, whether that was fur or the ground, bodies twisting, contorting, all for the passion that could only truly be experienced between mates that knew each other as well as they did.

His breath caught, chuffing, snarling, loins tightening. Selsei's cock had to be drooling, even as it lay inside her, pounding her, his mate ramming down onto him with greater and greater ferocity. For she wanted that cream of his seed as much as he wanted to spend it, filling her up to the brim, seeing her swell, the fertility of her coming to the surface as Akina so very much deserved. It was all needed, for the two of them, for the good of their bloodlines, though they had not seen any of their cubs since they had reached adulthood and, over time, struck out on their own.

But it was the way of it as he admired his mate's passion, how she slammed down on him, treating his body more roughly than he would have treated hers, even when deep in lust. His barbs had to be catching as his nuts tingled strangely, warm on the precipice of orgasm, panting harshly. She didn't care, however, not if the pain was burning through her, grinding down, taking him deep, Akina's eyes locking with Selsei's, daring him to breed her.

He could not resist. With a screaming yowl that sliced through the sky like his claws through the hide of a prey mammal, he ejaculated, humping up, scrabbling for any kind of purchase. Ropes of thick seed poured forth, pump after quick pump, for even in their land and world, they had to cum quickly, to not linger too long. They may have been apex predators but there were still other predators out there, other sabre-toothed tigers too looking for a chance, seeking to usurp. Not that Selsei would allow anyone to take or hurt Akina, but there was always that chance, his body knowing that and seeking out the shortest course of passionate action despite all else.

That was why it was good to have her pussy clenching and rippling around him, milking his dick, taking his orgasm in turn with hers. Her pleasure was paramount, but he needed it too, Akina's purrs rolling over him as pulse after twitch of climax and delight washed over him. His orgasm may have been swift to fade but her passion was not, the wetness of her cunny teasing around him, tempting and pulling, tail twitching, everything coming together in a burst of ecstasy. Selsei collapsed back with a low grunt and chuff, legs splayed out, his mate giggling on top of him, every part his queen but, irrefutably, his lover too.

"To think the king can be reduced to a purring little kitten with the right pussy…"

He growled, but was not about to get up, not with her heat wrapped around him, barbs easing down, cock softening, slowly and surely. It would not be quick to slide back into its sheath, not if his mate had anything to say about it, though he needed to rest, her lust teasing him, the mixture of their sexual juices slickening his cock to a lustful sheen.

The sabre-toothed tigers, however, had all the time in the world to enjoy one another, Akina taking her space on top of him, tail twitching, relaxing down into his warmth. Sharing the heat of their bodies, she soothed him with her purrs, letting his cock very slowly ease from her, no rush at all in their languid, soft, smooth movement.

The moment was theirs, his seed already working away deep inside her. Soon, she would show the evidence of their tryst, her belly swelling with new life.

Selsei trembled softly.

What more could he want from a moonlight mating?

# Seeding Her

"Oh, Cad..."

Trinity moaned, the grey-furred husky flat out on her back with her legs in the air. She was not alone there, in her bedroom, as her boyfriend stepped between her legs, his shaft teasing the outer lips of her pussy.

But Cad was not about to hold back from her, no, not as he slid his cock deep, the wolf's prick sinking into her wet heat as if it belonged there. He was bigger than her, a little burlier around the shoulders especially, with a thicker fluff of brown, russet and white fur, the colours blending softly into one another. Yet that was one thing, at least physically, she loved about him, feeling as if she was small enough before him that she needed to be taken care of, even though the husky could more than look after herself, whenever needed.

Yet he was sweet and he was kind and he had even got off work that afternoon to come over to help her out, as she'd been so worked up and horny. It was not Cad's fault that he worked a different shift pattern to her but Trinity had been just about to head down to his workplace herself to find a way to get a quickie in if he had not taken the initiative to plead an emergency and take the afternoon off.

It was not something, not by any means, that the wolf should get in the habit of doing, but, well...it was good to be young and dumb sometimes. It wasn't like anyone was going to find out about what he really had been doing anyway, so they could take a little risk.

But there was more risk too as Trinity grunted, squeezing her legs around his waist as she dragged him to her, wanting his cock driven deep, the knot swollen and lodged well within the bounds of her sensitive pussy. That feral need had not come upon her for a while, but there was only so much she could do when the needs of anthros, creatures like herself, sometimes came above even the pills they used to suppress their heat cycles.

Sometimes, those pills failed. Sometimes, their heat cycles were so powerful that they fell prey to them, needing to breed and even acting more feral in the heat of the moment, only knowing the lust of what their body craved.

And she realised too late, with his prick inside her, that she was in heat. She had to be, drooling for him as she was, her pussy so wet that she was slick and sloppy around the fat length of his dick. Cad leaned over her a little, tipping forward only slightly, one of his paws sliding down her leg to her thigh, rubbing soft circles into her grey fur at the point where it blended into the white.

"Mmmmm… Trin… Trinity," he breathed, though didn't slow the pump of his hips. "It's happened again, hasn't it? I'm going to have to pull out…ah…aren't I?"

She bubbled a laugh, arms flung back behind her head, the husky exulting in the moment. She almost didn't want to reply, not when it felt so good to be squeezing around him, trying to flex and pull her pussy along the length of his cock. Of course, Trinity did not possess that great control over her pussy, not in that way, but she still tried anyway.

She had to try, her lust rising, tongue lolling out as she licked her lips in a soft, sweet lap. She moaned and shook her head, coming back to herself only enough to answer his question.

"Ah… Mmmm… That…"

She struggled to get the words out, her boyfriend thrusting long and slow, sating her need with every stroke, even though the husky needed more, so much more.

"I… Yeah…" She panted heavily, finally settling for simple words, words she could get out more easily. "That's… That would be good…mmm…"

"Heh…" He smirked lightly, lips quirking up, and slowed his thrusts anymore. "Damn, should have realised before… Don't worry, Trin, I'll go real slow."

She didn't know what that meant, when he wanted to thrust deep, when he *should* have been thrusting deeper than ever. She didn't want him to go slow! Trinity wanted a real fuck, where his hips were bouncing off the flesh of her thighs and buttocks, the sound of their mating rising to fill the room.

It was risky, yes, but good risks were best taken with those they loved.

He panted as he looked down at her and she blushed faintly, though Trinity could not be too embarrassed by her current state. She was comfortable where she was, grunting thickly in the back of her throat, though it was all the husky could do not to let out all the weak whines and whimpers that wanted to break her lips. Her throat tightened with emotion, her pussy sliding along the length of his cock, desire pooling in the pit of her stomach.

Did Cad really know how much she needed him? Oh, she wasn't sure, not even as she arched up to meet him, using the leverage of her legs wrapped around his waist to pull herself up, just a little bit. There was only so much, after all, she could do in that regard, heavy pants raking their way through her chest as she whined and blinked, moisture trickling from the corners of her eyes.

"Oh… Mmm… Oh!"

Trinity did not mean to cry; it was just an overload of need getting the better of her. She clamped her jaws shut and shook her head back and forth as if she was trying to shake something off, but she couldn't shake off that manner of need. But it felt good, too good, to have him thrusting and grinding, slamming into her with every deep stroke, even though the wolf was still going far too slowly for her liking.

And then her eyes met those of the wolf's and she caught the edge of desperation in his gaze too, how he trembled with need against her, plunged as deeply into her pussy as he was able. There was no knot, not yet, but it threatened to swell, a little puffier at the base of his cock than it had been before.

"I know…this is risky…" The wolf puffed, leaning over her between her legs, his muzzle down close to hers. "But… Oh… Oh, Trinity…"

The husky squirmed, the sharp edge to his tone doing wonderful things to her. Oh, it made her wanted to climax right then and there, panting heavily, her pink tongue lolling happily from her muzzle.

"Stay inside me," she begged. "Oh… Cad… Please…"

"Come on, Trinity…" He groaned, licking her nose and drawing back. "It's okay, we can do other things. I've only got to look for a condom…"

And then he was pulling all the way back, his meat sliding from her sex as if he didn't intend to fuck her to completion as she wanted! She grunted, squirming and trying to clutch at him with her legs to keep him close to her, even if he couldn't be inside her at that very moment.

Yet the wolf was more sensible than she was and moved over the bed, next to her, taking up the space between the bed and the window, where the bed was pushed against the wall. It was their first home together and, well, they didn't have all that much room to move.

But that was okay for it was their own and they had everything they needed right there in that moment, as Trinity rolled on to her back and parted her legs for him all over again.

"Ah… Darling…" She whimpered, begging, pleading. "I need… More than your tongue…"

"I know, I know, but I'll get you off and then…mmm…we'll do something more, okay?"

As he moved over her, head to tail, his fluffy tail lifted and she grabbed his thighs, pulling him down on top of her. With him being larger than she was, they just about lined up with his dick able to slide between her lips, though that was mostly as seamless as it was because she was ready to receive him. Hungering for his dick, she lavished attention on it, swirling her tongue around the tip before taking it deep into the back of her throat, her cheeks puffing out from the effort it took to keep him there.

"Ah… Trinity…"

Her boyfriend shuddered, though it was not as if he was in a position to fight back against her, not when his need matched up with her own so perfectly. He panted hotly against her sex, his breath washing over her pussy, again and again, and she moaned for him, even though her words and cries were muffled around his shaft.

That was all she needed, to be there, taken, his cock shuddering within her mouth as he thrust slowly, taking her maw. Her tongue cradled his length and she squirmed delightedly, pushing her legs out even further than before, as Cad's wolfish tongue played over her pussy, stroking up the line of her sex and swirling around her clit. He panted against her sex and dipped his tongue inside her.

The wolf must have more than liked what he tasted, however, for he dug in readily, eating her out with a raw, feral abandonment that would have had Trinity thinking Cad too was in heat, if that was possible for males. Sure, they had breeding seasons and cycles that sometimes made them more randy, though they were not as stringent as the monthly cycle, in the warmer months of the year, was for femfurs.

Yet she adored it, wanting that. And why did she want it? When her blood sang and her heart pounded, she simply craved every stroke, every thrust, every deep push of his cock into her mouth. Yet the husky was only imagining that her mouth was her pussy, in that moment, wanting his dick inside her, ploughing her full.

And bare too... Oh, they had been together for more than long enough! Why would they ever have needed a condom? Even though it was a risk, it was a risk they could take for themselves, yes, all so she could be seeded, a hefty dose of his cream drooling from her pussy in a messy cream-pie.

He groaned above her as her tongue played over the sensitive glands of his cock, teasing and pleasing, though Trinity was only about coaxing her partner to fuck her properly again. That was all she needed, all she craved. And she had an inkling too that the wolf was as ready for it all as she was.

Sometimes, things just had to be taken. A leap of faith could be held close, both of them falling, together, arm in arm, a smile on their lips.

"Mmmmph... Nnngghhh..."

She groaned around his cock as her pussy dripped wetly, more and more spilling from her, though it was his tongue that dragged her arousal forth. He circled her clit and suckled it between his lips – and it was at that point the husky lost control. Howling and yelping around his cock, she flinched and jerked, thrusting up erratically against his glorious tongue, even as the tapered tip of his cock plunged into the back of her throat.

She gagged lightly on him but suppressed her gag reflex the best she could, just wanting him to spill his load. Not in her mouth, not even as orgasm rose and fell within her, giving her pulse after pulse of ecstasy, her body flooded with warmth. Yet it was only when the lure of orgasm fell once more, leaving her paddling in the overflowing afterglow, that she could speak again.

Cad pulled out of her mouth, checking in on her, but she pushed away his paw gently when he offered her water. Her eyes burned and she locked her gaze with his, taking a slow, deep breath.

"Cad… I want you…inside. Please."

The wolf's ears twitched and he let out a low whine, giving the tiniest shake of his head.

"Oh, Trin…" He whimpered, suddenly seeming smaller than he was, even as he leaned over her, bundling the dog up into his arms. "I want… Mmm… I want that too. But…do you think we're even ready for it?"

She challenged him with her stare, lips stretching, faintly, into an open-mouthed smile.

"Yeah… Yeah, I think we are. And I want you, only you, Cad. Please… Breed me. I want this, I want this so badly."

They should have, of course, taken more time to think about the whole thing and consider it, but there was only so much that could be done there. At least, they were openly in agreement as Cad growled possessively and nipped at her neck, holding her close as he pinned her to the bed in a mating press. His thighs came down over hers, pinning them to the mattress and holding them apart: it was the most dominant position Trinity could ever have thought of when it came to mating and breeding lust.

"Ah… Yes… Cad… Ah… Take me!"

She whined as his teeth caught her neck and the full length of his meat sank back into her hot and ready pussy, closing around him in a tight clench. Trinity moaned, her tail trying to wag back and forth even as she was held in place, her lover gently taking her paws and holding them both above her head. Of course, the canine could have wriggled free of that grasp if she'd really wanted to, though there was nothing to worry about there, just another nuance of faint kink that made her heart sing for him.

Finally... She was going to get what she needed. Her pussy ached as he ploughed her, claiming her in shorter, sharper, needier thrusts than before, as if the wolf was truly letting go with her for the very first time. His need was evident as he crammed the length of his cock into her, panting heavily against her neck, even as he nipped and nibbled at the point between her shoulder and her neck.

"Mmm..." He rumbled, pupils dilating, his knot finally starting to swell – but slowly enough that he could push in all the way so it could inflate inside her if wanted. "Mine... You're all mine, only mine."

*Yes... Yes, my love...*

She drifted, rising and falling on a sea of passion that came and went, prey to emotion, the needs of her body. And it was what she'd wanted all along, of course, to fall that far and to let it all throb through her oh so very deliciously, so she didn't have to worry about anything at all, nor think of anything.

It was better that way, just to let her body dictate what came next, breathlessly whimpering her partner's name, though Trinity barely even remembered her own in that moment. All she knew was that his thick length inside her was all she needed, how he stretched her pussy to the perfect amount, their bodies designed to come together in exactly the right way.

"Mmm… Nnngghhhh… Ohhhhh!"

She moaned and bucked her hips – or, at least, she tried to. Another orgasm crashed through her and she was aware of his knot swelling again, the raised edge of it grinding against her pussy. He'd have to push in, or not, in the next few moments or else he would be too large to fit her.

"Ah… Trinity… Are you sure?"

She nodded fervently, letting out a plaintive whine, ecstasy throbbing through her, stealing her ability to speak. Yet Cad knew and understood exactly what it was she wanted and gripped her fingers tightly, linking his with hers, as he ground deeply enough for his knot to swell all the way, locking them together.

From that point, there really was no going back as he grunted thickly, tail lifting proudly in breeding lust. Cad took her in short, driving strokes, the pump of his hips speeding up into a frenzy she'd never seen before. Yet it was just what they wanted, everything they'd needed, their lives set to change in the beat of a heart – as another heartbeat was due to join their shared lives together.

"Unff… Ah… Mine… My Trinity."

He growled, biting her shoulder and leaving a mark under her fur as, finally, orgasm took him and another rolled through Trinity, though she was barely locked in to her own sense of reality in that moment. She howled and lost herself on waves of lust, acutely aware of every hot spurt of cum that splattered up inside her pussy, seeding her full, giving her every drop of cream that she had needed from the wolf for so very long.

And all she could do was languish there, relaxing in the moment, whining and pressing her muzzle against that of her partner, for she was right where she needed to be. The wolf would remain there, tied with her, for as long as it took his knot to soften – which could be anywhere from fifteen to thirty minutes, give or take, in her experience. And she would be there, of course, taking every spurt and trickle of cum he had to give her, not a drop of it able to escape her pussy.

The knot ensured her pregnancy – well, there was always a risk she wouldn't fall pregnant. But she wanted to, very much, and she would take it all, everything he wanted to give her, as her wolf's arms slid down around her, cradling her to his chest.

"Mmm… I love you so much."

Cad panted softly, bathing the spot on her shoulder that he'd bitten with his tongue, though there was plenty of time for them to relax together. There was nothing to rush them, not as they settled and he rolled on to his back, drawing her with him, all so he could let her rest on top and no longer be held under his form.

Their lives were going to change, but, as their decision was made, there would be many more breeding sessions for them both to enjoy until they got that sweet, positive pregnancy test.

# Massage

It was not usual to find an anthro zebra and giraffe pairing in Wales, even close to the border to England, though Liza and Chima had found one another regardless. He'd just been passing through, travelling for work, though they'd struck up conversation in a service station on the motorway, of all places – and that had been it for them. Even though they lived some distance apart, they found a way to make things work, staying in touch and connecting even when it was not all that easy just to pop around to one of their apartments without planning ahead.

But things could still be planned and a long weekend tucked away in Liza's Cardiff apartment was just what they needed, the rain hammering down within the cosy walls, lashing the windows with a dark fury as if it was trying to strike its way inside.

"Just relax, darling, there's nothing you need to worry about…"

His accent tremored, the zebra's soft lips twitching faintly as he leaned over his lover's back, hands sweeping up on either side of her spine. That was one massage technique, letting himself sink and melt into the motion, pushing against the natural smoothness of the body, he'd learned back in Africa, but it had been a long time since he'd lived there full time. He'd gone back, with his family, for many holidays and, of course, to further some of his studies too, called by something deeper, something more instinctive. The lure of his homeland, after all, was marked deep into his bones.

Liza, however, had been born in England and moved to Wales, so things were a little different for her, despite them both talking about taking a trip over to Africa to visit important sites to them and their families. It was simply that easy for them to plan their future together, the long-legged giraffe matching up with the zebra as if they'd been fated to meet.

"Mmm…"

Liza did her best to relax into it, though there was a sense of invigoration about her too, her tail swinging back and forth over the edge of the massage table. To think he had even bought a massage table and had it delivered to her! It was a good thing there was plenty of space in her apartment, partly as she hadn't spent too much time there, always out and about for work and seeing friends.

Chima too, of course. She felt like she'd barely spent any time there, even as he shared the space with her, when she wanted to be in her zebra's arms, the sanctity of touch teasing in closer and closer.

So, Chima had transformed her spare bedroom into a relaxing oasis, the storage wardrobe all closed up and all the mess in there tucked away (not much had been needed anyway, what had been there regardless). It had left more than enough space for him to set up candles on the shelf, burning and flickering with dancing flames, the massage table taking pride of place right in the centre of the room.

His phone cast music to the small sound system he'd set up in there, with a good speaker so it felt like the music was surrounding them, and Liza's ears twitched as she settled a little more, moments of relaxation nipping at her hide.

*He even cleaned in here…*

She really thought he'd thought of everything. However could someone care for her so much that he thought of every little detail? She barely even knew what that meant, her breath hitching and catching, though the giraffe tried to still the languid sway of her tail.

Her need came out through her tail, though, of course, she was naked on the table. She didn't need to wear clothing around her zebra, not as he warmed her skin and patterned coat of hair with infused oils. Chima had told her what the oils were and their properties, but, well, she'd forgotten what they were. It didn't matter and that kind of information just didn't seem to lodge itself in her mind all that readily.

"Mmm… Oh, Chima…"

She shook her head faintly, shaking out the kinks in her neck, though his hands slid up her back to the back of her neck, kneading and massaging gently. Just how Chima's fingers pressed into her flesh pulled down and made her want to lean even more into her touch than she was already, a shudder of need rippling through her.

No… She had to hold back, to see what Chima had in store for her. It was not on Liza, after all, to interrupt his plans, the soft, soothing nature of his hands sweeping over her hide.

A towel covered her, though her tail twitched at it, her buttocks hidden while her breasts pressed softly into the padded top of the table.

"You're as tense as always," he murmured, the low note of his voice dripping like warmed honey. "Hm… I should be here more often."

"Mmm…" Liza agreed. "We should find somewhere else though… Somewhere we can both put our stamp on the place."

Chima blinked, but she didn't catch that little hesitation, even though the zebra wasn't entirely sure what the phrase meant. That was okay, however, as Chima relaxed into the motion, putting a little more weight into it as he worked his way into her shoulders and between the shoulder blades, pausing briefly there.

"Mmmm…"

Her warming hum was everything he needed, the zebra's nose quivering faintly, soft and velvety as they wobbled. He eased down lightly, shaking his head, though his upright mane jiggled faintly on top of his neck, trimmed into a neat line.

She was beautiful and he yearned for her, wearing only a long pair of shorts. The apartment was more than warm enough for him to ease into the moment without shivering, though he preferred warmer places, as a general rule. Liza was a little better used to wrapping up warmly than he was when the weather was inclement, though he managed better in the summer.

Maybe she could be the one to warm him through the winter months again? If they could find a way to spend more time together. The distance was not all that great, but he grunted softly, clenching his jaw.

It might not have been much, but it was enough to make things more difficult for them, his hips rocking faintly as he adjusted his weight. He just wanted to see her every day, to come home to her after work, though even the drudgery of work was something else indeed.

It was time for a change for both of them, though there was only so much they could do. With the rain coming down hard, streaming down the streets and into the gutters, the night was for them – and not for any worries.

Connection was to be had there, in the moment, taking a deep breath as he ran his fingers over her ribs – what he could reach from the back of her body, at least. There was so much sensitive skin and fascia there that needed attention and he dragged his fingers, applying light friction, though his hoof-like, hard fingertips were challenging even then. He had to be gentler with her and Liza's thin skin did not play well with a harder, rougher touch.

She was, however, sensitive as he teased her skin, running his fingers more lightly back up to the outside edge of her shoulders, though Chima was applying more of an intuitive massage that time. Maybe another time he would study more techniques to really target those points of stress and soreness in her body, though he'd learned from touch and feel.

There was always more to be built on and the zebra chuffed lowly as he admired her body. Her shoulders were strong and broad and he was not embarrassed at all to admit she was a good foot and a half taller than he was, especially considering her neck. Most giraffes tended to be on the taller side, yet Liza had a way about her that didn't make it feel at all as if she was looming over him.

They were partners. They were equal. That had always been the most important thing to him.

Chima licked his lips, eyes tracing lines down her back, though the zebra was no longer entirely focused on his massage.

Liza shifted under his hands as he reached lower, toying with the top of the towel, which covered her buttocks. Not that she minded him slipping it away from her, not in the slightest, but she wanted to do more, her skin prickling and tingling, invigorated and alive.

It was where she needed to be, taking deep breath after breath, settling into place. She didn't need to move, not yet, not when he was taking such good care of her. But she ached for more, warm between the thighs even though the zebra's hands had not yet gone down there in the slightest.

"Mmm…" Perhaps she would have to be the one to make the first move, after all, catching the hitch in his breath. "Hon…"

"Mm?" His voice was soft, breathy, as if he was trying to be quiet and not disturb the peace of the room, the light scents complementing one another sweetly in the air. "Is there anything more I can do for you?"

Even with her face tucked neatly into the hole in the table, watching his legs shift and Chima's tail swing, Liza chuckled faintly. It was like being in a whole other world down there, her view of the world changing as she adjusted her weight, rocking from one hip to the other. Yet the giraffe could see something down there the zebra perhaps had not accounted for.

"Mmm, I think you know, you want it too…"

She hinted at it, though kept a soft eye on the shift and rise in his shorts. He was not fully aroused, not by a long shot, but enough that he moved a little more awkwardly, his shorts tugging and catching over the head of his cock where it was fleshing out and filling out from his sheath.

Chima chuckled, ears twitching. Ah, she was astute, though the massage was never intended to be purely chaste, no, not by a long shot. And that was okay too, for he was more than eager to go with the flow of things, to take things where they needed to be.

He slid his hands down her body, sliding the towel off and out of the way, his hooves braced a little further apart than before. His sheath tightened around his shaft, though it stretched nicely to accommodate his length, though Chima had not expected to be that aroused so swiftly. It was just too easy when he was leaning over his giraffe, a flare of possessiveness nestled in the pit of his stomach.

She was his and not his, her own creature at the same time… And he didn't want to stop her from achieving everything in life she set her mind to, no, not in the slightest. On the contrary, he wanted to see just how far she could fly, a smile on her lips and her arms spread wide, welcoming the change of the day.

But that was why he had to savour every moment with her, to live like he was trying to remember everything, present there in his own sliver of reality. He ran his fingers over her glutes softly, pressing in, and the zebra's cock plumped out a little more, slowly thickening and rising with a flush of raw need.

"Mmm…"

She was gorgeous, but there was so much more to her than that, her personality shining through wonderfully, all in the very best of ways. He swore he even caught it in the twitch of Liza's ears, how she gave that subtle intake of breath, her shoulder blades pushing back towards him, though only for a fraction of a moment.

"I think you want more than just to please me here, my zebra…"

Her croon caught his attention and Chima grinned, not hiding anything anymore.

"Oh, how did you realise?"

"Hm…" Liza obviously pretended to ponder, sliding her head up and back out of the hole in the massage table, just to cast him a flirtatious look. "Maybe the fact you're filling out your shorts with something special for me, hon?"

The zebra chuckled and her heart lifted for him. That was a thing only he could do for her, though it would take Liza longer still before she admitted that to him. There were layers to her, after all, and a part of her which still wanted to guard herself, not allowing herself to reveal too much all at once.

That was coming, however, slowly and surely. Bit by bit, she opened up to him, allowing him to ease into the moment with her as he rubbed over her buttocks, stepping down to the bottom of the massage table. There was, after all, no reason at all for Chima to hold back in the slightest as he exhaled softly, his lips wobbling as he massaged down her glutes and the tops of her thighs, an intimate caress that could only be spent between the two of them.

"Mmmm…"

She hummed lightly, under her breath, though the giraffe could not help but spread her legs just a little more for the zebra. And when his fingers brushed the folds of her pussy, wet with the faintest gleam of moisture, well… She was already lost to him.

Her tail lifted and she accepted his touch, her body aching for him, heart pounding. Something pulled at the back of her mind, reminding her there was something she was forgetting – but, funnily enough, Liza couldn't bring that to her mind, not at that moment.

*Shoot…*

The giraffe groaned, rolling her shoulders back, her breath catching. Dealing with heats was not the kind of thing many anthros had to deal with anymore, but there were some cycles, sometimes as they were moving into the warmer months of the year, that caught female furs off-guard. However, it was Autumn, not Spring or Summer, and the giraffe had not been anticipating something like that in the slightest.

*In heat… Damn it…*

Her head fogged but Liza leaned into how simply good it felt to have him there with her, both wrapped up in their little oasis, where only the two of them existed. There was nothing there to bother them, not as tickling fingers of heat pulled through her body, pooling and coiling in her loins.

"Mmmmm… Ah!"

She shuddered bodily as Chima caressed her folds, sliding a finger inside her when she had not been expecting it. Yet she gripped his finger as tightly with her sex as she could, her pussy hot and wet, even if his finger felt like a spear of tension grinding deep into her. That was right, yes, the way it was supposed to be, her own breath warm on her lips, nostrils flaring and puckering, striving with all their might to draw in all the breath they needed for her suddenly aching lungs.

Every part of her body ached and, with a shudder, she pushed herself up, the muscle in her arms contracting, lips faintly parted. Startled, Chima jostled back from her, ears twitching, yet it was not up to him what the moment entailed – not as Liza slid to the ground before him, smoothly and sinuously as if she had planned the whole thing all along.

"Ah – Liza?"

Yet the giraffe was fuelled by desire in that moment, something she couldn't quite hold back from when her partner was as willing as he was. The zebra's cock tented out even more of the front of his shorts than before and her heart leapt in her chest at the treat she was just about to enjoy, stroking her fingers up the underside of his length – or what she could see of it, at least, through his shorts.

"Mmmph… Ah, Liza…"

He moaned, ears splaying out and nose twitching softly. He didn't have the heart to tell her to stop, though he leaned into it. There was a strange smell in the air, something he hadn't caught from her before – something that reminded him of how a femfur zebra smelled when she was in season. He didn't know if the time was quite right to ask if that was what was going on with Liza right then and there, but he kept it in the back of his mind.

They wouldn't want to take any risks, after all, no. That wasn't a step they'd discussed in their relationship and they'd been careful with both birth control pills and condoms. Heats, of course, usually surpassed the contraceptive pill when they came into effect, the mix of hormones at work too potent for anything anthros had come up with so far.

That was probably why femfurs were still cautious of them: for good reason.

But it was hard not to linger there as she caressed the shape of his cock, gripping him with her fingers through his shorts. Yet it was no time at all before Liza had the zebra's shaft out and in her hand, licking her lips as she slid his shorts down.

"Out of these…"

There was a breathy note in her voice, but he still went along with it, his heart pounding so hard in his chest that it felt like each pound of it reverberated through his whole body. He'd set up the night to adore and pamper her, but Liza had taken matters well and truly into her own hands – which, to be fair, Chima should have expected. It was one thing he loved so deeply about his wonderful giraffe and he never would have ever wanted to suppress that part of her.

"Mmm, Liza…"

She caressed his shaft as he stepped obligingly out of his shorts, not wanting those to get in the way either, not as he grunted and huffed. His ropey tail swayed behind him, but the zebra held back from flicking it as his meaty length swelled fully into her touch.

It was always a strange sensation to feel his cock plumping out with blood, the medial ring defined as the wrinkles and creases mostly smoothed out. His cock was on the larger side, being a zebra, and hung down slightly under its own weight, trying to point to the ground in a gentle curve. Of course, Liza was there to hold his dick up as she played her tongue over the flatter, fleshier head, making him shudder and twitch as she stoked the embers of pleasure.

"Mmmm… Oh…"

Chima groaned as Liza slid her lips over the head of his cock, not yet flared, and suckled faintly, closing her lips just behind the glands. She didn't need to go further than that, not yet – and, frankly, Chima didn't expect her to do more. She always liked to tease him so much and he stomped a hoof, his tail swishing without ample direction from his mind, trying his best to relax into the moment, just so he didn't lose control of his already pleasantly warming nuts too quickly. They swung faintly as his sack hung down, the skin covering them delicate and almost velvety, though Chima had heard that said about others, rather than it being something the zebra said about himself.

"Agh!"

He trembled, rolling his hips forward – though Chima really did not need to do that as the giraffe engulfed his cock in the hungry heat of her wet mouth. He hadn't expected that, not in the slightest, and stayed there, shaking bodily, his skin twitching and juddering as if he was trying to shake off flies. Yet the zebra grappled with himself, his fingers going to her head and winding into her brown hair, though she kept it shorter than most. There was enough there for him to just about pull his fingers through it, enough to grip, and his heart leapt in his chest, beating harder and faster as blood roared in his ears.

She had to be in heat, but it already felt like things were going too far for them to do nothing at all. Chima groaned, swallowing a very zebra-like bray. Damn it… He should have waited, should have checked with Liza first, but female furs barely even got their heats anymore!

He shifted his weight, though it was not all that hard to resign himself to the lure of oral pleasure, his massage taking a more intimate twist, focused on him that time. For there was no other way to play out the moment or describe the smooth tease of her fleshy, long tongue on the underside of his cock. For her tongue was much larger than his was, dark and sinuous, able to curl and wrap around his cock, dragging back down the full length in a teasingly intimate massage that had Chima's head spinning.

"Agh… Ohhhhhh, fuck!"

He was not always one to curse, not like that, though the zebra couldn't help himself as he shifted his weight from hoof to hoof, his tail swinging to his back. It thwapped heavily into the backs of his thighs but even that was not something he could control, not as he tried not to thrust, not to spear deeply into her mouth.

No… That would be crude. Especially when Liza was as wrapped up as she was in sucking his cock, playing her tongue around the rising flare, betraying the true depth of his need even in that moment. Her hands even came up, sliding confidently over the muscle of his thighs, caressing his nuts and weighting them in her hands as if she was anticipating, even then, a load of cum to rise from them.

*Ah… I can't…*

The zebra quivered, her mouth so slick around his cock, the giraffe taking him deep into her throat. And, oh, how he loved that bulge in her throat, how it swelled out, though Liza skilfully took him deep as if it was no trouble at all to her. Her throat pulled around him as she gulped and Chima nearly lost control right then and there, his vision blurring – yet only for the briefest of moments.

At least with her blowing him, there was no risk of her getting pregnant from that, no. But maybe that was a reason he had to hold back, his head swimming with pleasant feelings, endorphins flooding his mind. It was so hard not to rock his hips – though maybe spending himself down her throat was the right way to go too?

*Think, Chima!*

"Mmm…"

Yet all that left his lips was a groan, eyes cast down adoringly on the giraffe before him. Did Liza even know how hot she was?

"Ah… Liza…" He tugged at her hair, trying to get her to pay attention to him, though she dredged herself back up slowly, lips pulling so very slickly up the full length of his erection. "You've got to… Do you know?"

She suckled fervently at the tip of his cock as she pulled back, looking up at him accusingly.

"Mmm, what?" She said, clicking her tongue wetly against the roof of her mouth. "Honestly, Chima… You're spoiling my fun."

She cast him a look but didn't really mean her words, not in a bad way. Yet not even Liza could say there wasn't a hot wash of need layering heavily through her tone, as if it was trying to add a sultry note to everything, even the shift and set of her body.

"You're…" Oh, he was so cute with that blush in his cheeks, struggling to find the words as she stared up at him, her fingers curled around as much of the base of his shaft as they could. "You're in heat, Liza, aren't you? We can't…"

The giraffe rolled her eyes and shook her head.

"Oh, you can't mean that, Chima, we will be careful," she implored him, the edges of her mind fuzzy with need. "I want you… We'll be careful, so careful…"

He was easy to persuade, though it was not as if it was a singular decision. Either the zebra or the giraffe could stop things at any time and no one was being forced – but the lure of one's heat was so tantalising. It even affected Chima, of course, as her body released more pheromones, though that was not something, honestly, either of them had paid all that much attention to in the past.

So, the giraffe suckled on his cock again like it was the finest treat in the world, her hand between her thighs, massaging and groping her pussy. Yet Liza couldn't seem to get her fingers in the right place at the right time, puffing out sharp breaths of air in her frustration, everything so soft and hazy around her.

"Mmmph…"

Losing herself, she groaned around him, eyes watering as she looked up at her zebra. She wanted him… She needed him… And from the twitching set and shiver of his body, Chima wanted her just as badly.

Would a little bit hurt, really?

"Mmm, Chima…" She breathed, pulling back of her own accord that time, though Liza could not stop herself from lapping over the head of his cock between utterances. "I want you… We'll be careful, okay? Just get a condom…"

She didn't recall that they'd run out last time, that she'd had to throw out an expired box. But it sounded like a reasonable idea to her, in the heat of the moment.

So, she climbed back up on to the massage table, her legs hanging over the edge, grunting as she masturbated and he headed off to find the condoms. Yet Liza didn't catch him scuffling and muttering, checking his bags too, looking in the usual spots for the condoms – and, of course, not finding anything at all. She was too busy trying to work out why masturbating didn't feel as good as it usually did. Of course, there was pleasure there, but there was something else too, a rampant, driving need deep in the pit of her belly that Chima had set off for her.

He returned, however, to find her with a hand wet with her own arousal between her thighs and a truly desperate look on her face. Liza stared him down with glassy eyes, her breasts rising and falling sharply with every breath. Small and neat on her lithe body, every grab at air her lungs made rolled up through her breasts and, for a moment, that was all the zebra could look at, even if he had more serious things he had to tell her.

"I don't have a condom this time…" He muttered softly, ears splaying. "I can't find any of them. Agh… Liza, I'm sorry."

"We can risk it."

His ears perked and he looked at her, a gleam in his eye even as his hide quivered softly.

"What do you mean?"

Oh, it was alluring, but Chima didn't want to get the wrong impression, no, not in the slightest. But it was hard to interpret that special little look in her eye as anything other than truth and honesty, the giraffe meaning everything she said.

"I…"

He couldn't get the words out, so Liza took charge for him. Hooking a leg around him, she dragged him to her (only grateful later that the wheels on the massage table were locked), his cock bouncing off her thigh.

"I'm willing to risk it," she murmured, a twinge of knowing need bubbling inside her. "If you are. Only if you are."

For the giraffe was not mindless, no, even if her body wanted something desperately that she had not anticipated needing to satisfy that night. And that was his cock inside her, yes, even if they could find other ways, something else to do.

"I…" Chima grunted, nostrils flaring, though his lips were already twitching up in a smile. "Um… It should be easy, right? Mmmph… It'll be okay, I'll just pull out?"

"Yes, yes…" She gasped, Chima lining up between her legs as she hooked both legs around him, crossing her ankles behind his back, her cloven hooves dangling at his glutes. "You'll pull out, we'll pay attention. I just need it a little bit, Chima, just a little. I want *you* more than that."

Yet they were finding ways to justify what they so clearly wanted from one another, though the two of them would only find out about more driving, feral breeding urges afterwards. Their fate was already sealed and it was for the best they had each other as he pressed the head of his cock to her soaked folds.

There were no words in Chima's mind or on his lips as he kept eye contact with the giraffe, slowly grinding inside her in a long, drawn-out thrust. It took every ounce of self-control he had in him, but he wanted to give her every chance to say "no," to tell him to pull out again. He had to be aware, though his stomach churned with raw need, knowing he was where he needed to be.

Who knew that a minor risk like that could be so *hot*?

"Unff…"

He thrust slowly, savouring every moment, for Chima feared spoiling it all if he went too roughly and too hard too quickly. He had to drag it out, to give her what she needed, his hand down at the front of her pussy, clumsily seeking her clit. The giraffe under him arched up, grinding deeply on to his cock, his vision exploding with stars as his eyelids swept down.

"Ah… Oh, Liza!"

She was amazing, every inch of her, from head to hoof. Her tail flicked down over the edge of the table and he gripped her right buttock with his hand, fingertips digging in lusciously to her soft flesh. Yet it was both of them there, rocking together, his cock driving into her harder and more roughly, losing control.

They were in it together, even as she grabbed for him, her fingers on his arm, still wet with her juices. There was no denying, not in the slightest, their shared need, not as their breath hitched and caught, as if other parts of their body were being more challenged than ever in that moment, their pleasure paramount above all else.

Or maybe it was just the breeding urges at play, all as Chima ground in deeply, the massage table shifting and even creaking a little under their weight. He was, after all, bearing over it more and more as he thrust, seemingly not as able to control himself as the zebra had expected.

But it was fine… They'd agreed he would pull out and he would do that. Even if perhaps a part of them both knew there was no way that was going to happen.

Liza's moans carried him onward, spearing deep, again and again, her pussy gripping him with every stroke of his cock. How could she be as slick as she was and still give him that delicious, sweet friction? His moans rose and the zebra's hide quivered in delight, the flare of his shaft thickening more and more.

"Mmph… Liza…" He breathed, grunting out the words the best he could. "I'm kinda…close…"

He knew it was soon, but that couldn't be helped after the mind-blowing blowjob she'd given him already. Yet Liza was not ready to let him pull out, shaking her head and whining as he nodded, understanding he was to keep going. He could hold off a little longer, Chima was sure, if he was careful. The zebra just had to be really focused on what he was doing, powering into the giraffe's slick pussy with sharp, juddering thrusts, focused on her pleasure above his own.

At some point, however, his hand had drifted from her pussy, for it was not needed anymore. Not with every fibre of her being and nerve ending in her body quivering with devout breeding need, aching for one thing and one thing alone.

It was only up to Chima to give it to her, to quench the fire in the giraffe's body as they were meant to. He slammed in, huffing and panting, not even realising he had sped up, a little dizzy with the overload of pleasure thrumming through his body. The zebra's tail swung and, before he knew it, Liza arched up against him, dragging him in as deep as he could possibly go, a feeling like a lurch rolling through his nuts.

She had not even realised she was that close, pulling him in hard as orgasm ripped her from reality, rooting her merely in sensation, where she belonged. The most explosive orgasm of her life tore through her and the giraffe could have sobbed for the relief it brought her, her pussy clenching around him, rippling and pulling. Yet that was not in her control, even as Liza had enough presence of mind to just about loosen the grip of her legs on him, knowing in some faint, sensible part of her mind, that they had gone as far as they could go. At least that time.

Yet, to her euphoria and surprise, Chima did not pull out, the zebra's eyes suddenly widening as her pussy caressed his length, the twitches and ripples not something she could stop. He juddered – and brayed aloud, cock half inside her as if he had been trying to pull back at the very moment climax rolled through him.

And yet there was nothing they could do about it, caught in the moment of trying to ensure he did not spend his seed bare inside her, ropes of thick, creamy zebra seed flooding her pussy. He groaned and thrust, a chuff breaking his lips, but Chima did not plough fully into her, containing himself faintly, though he spent his load inside her, nonetheless.

Need pooled inside her – the kind of desire that could not be sated by anything else, so she moaned and hopelessly tightened her legs around him, drawing the zebra's cock in deep.

They were in it together, so the pair revelled in the pleasure together, even if such a deep massage could only roll into one outcome. Their eyes met and they simmered there, relaxing into it, the bubble of a confused chuckle behind Chima's lips. It was a moment unlike any other, some of his seed drooling out of her pussy where their bodies joined, dribbling down her folds and over the pucker of her tail.

Yet it was to be remembered too, settling there, knowing they'd passed that point of no return and determining to enjoy the moment. For she was there for every throb of his cock inside her, the flare dragging lightly through her pussy – and Chima relished in how her pussy clenched around him, the rippling aftershocks of orgasm still there to caress and tug at his cock, as if her body thought he had even more to give her. They wouldn't be daring enough to risk another round of sex, not with his cock inside her, but, well…the damage there had already been done. If it could even be called that.

In the end, it was worth it: they both said the same. With the candlelight flickering, something beautiful happened in the shift of life, bringing them closer together than ever before.

Things changed, but only for the better as her belly rose and rose with the swell of new life. Finally, they were able to close the distance between them, glad of the push for them to do so.

Perhaps Chima and Liza should have waited a little longer before having a calf (or foal, depending on who was talking about the baby), though, for them, everything worked out exactly the way it was meant to.

Still, they'd always remember the raunchy little massage that turned the course of their path together forever…

# Glowing

Jason smiled, the bull leaning back in the bath with his pregnant partner in his arms, sitting with her back to his chest. Although he had not honestly anticipated ending up in a relationship with a member of his own species, Jason didn't want things to be any other way than how they were. His sweet cow was the light of his life, even though his buddies had teased him for being as infatuated with her as he was, but, well…that only meant he was head over (cloven) hooves for her.

And why would the elk have wanted things to be any different than that? They were perfect, or his version of perfect, even if there were still challenges in their relationship.

Yet…he could sink into the moment from time to time as he breathed in slowly and deeply, evening out his breath so Olivia, his cow, was pulled along with him. The calmer he was, the easier things were, for their energy played in tune with one another most of the time. It was why she was always, so far, able to calm him down after a bad day at work, stilling the frenzied storm in his chest when he thought things there couldn't be any more chaotic.

Yeah… Jason grimaced lightly, his ears twitching. He'd have to see about changing his job at some point, but he wanted to work through her pregnancy and at least the first year of their calf being born so they had secure finances. It was terribly boring and droll to think about things like that when they should both have merely been looking forward to the big change in their lives, but sometimes needs simply worked out that way.

With the big things taken care of, they had to settle and relax into the moment, letting everything else pass them by.

At least for a little while.

Olivia sighed softly, swilling her fingers through the water and bubbles, her eyes barely open. Peering at the bathroom from under lowered eyelashes, she shook her head minutely, marvelling at how her husband had changed things so swiftly in the bathroom, without her even being at all aware of what Jason had been planning. He'd built a new cabinet and fastened it to the wall already, so all clutter was neatly tidied away, even fixed the faulty window latch too. However, the more romantic note came in the candles he'd lit around the room, all with her favourite scents mingling: lavender and bergamot. The first reminded her of her mother and the second, well, just hit a deep part of her soul, helping her take deep, calming breaths, settling herself and her mind.

Her large, pregnant belly rose before her, swelling out above the surface of the water. The bubbles framed her stomach and Olivia giggled faintly, barely a whisper on her breath. Her paw swept over her stomach, the cow's brown fur glistening with moisture, damp with a soft sheen to it.

"Pregnancy really makes you glow, darling…"

She blushed and wriggled, squirming back against his naked body. Yet it was far more comfortable for the elk in the bath than it was elsewhere, the water helping support the weight of her heavily pregnant belly.

"Mmm… That's so sweet of you, honey," she breathed, closing her eyes and settling a little deeper back into the cup of his arms and torso. "I feel like a whale though. It's so heavy…"

"Darling, you could never be a whale," he hastened to assure her, though Olivia held back her giggle, not having meant it all that seriously. "You're beautiful, I want you to know that every day."

"Mmm…" She pretended to ponder that, wriggling back against him a little more. "Even when I have stretch marks?"

He kissed the back of her head, his lips lingering there a moment longer than anticipated as Olivia shivered.

"Even more so then, I promise."

His fingers traced a path down from her arm to her hip, resting there, lightly curled around. The cow's breath caught but she tried not to be too obvious about it, heat warming her through – though, that time, it was not from the bath, not even from the delectable warmth of the water sinking into her flesh and bones.

It was so much more than that. She glanced back lightly at him from the corner of her eye, opening her eyes a little wider than before, though only to take in her husband.

He was strong, though retained a lean, agile elk-like quality to him. Of course, the bull could never be confused for any species other than what he was with a big rack of antlers, sixteen proud tines rising high. His shoulders were narrower than some but rounded out with muscle, moderately toned throughout his body. After doing long-distance running in his younger years, the bull had kept up going to the gym, though he was not the sort who went for heavy lifting or the like. Jason just wanted to keep active and fit, so he could be the best version of himself for Olivia and himself too he could be.

Olivia, however, secretly thought there was a little vanity there too. But who should never have fallen prey to a touch of vanity, after all? Not everything was a bad thing and looking after himself meant her dear bull could look after her better too.

So, everything worked. And she hoped she would be able to care for him as he cared for her.

Yet Olivia could not hide her need from him, the bull's lips twitching in the corner as he held her closer, sliding his fingers tentatively down her thigh, in closer to her pussy, moment by moment. Yet Jason didn't have to rush, no, not at all, knowing she couldn't see him as he rubbed his fingers and paw back and forth, as if it was all merely a coincidence his paw had ended up down there at just the right time.

"Mmm…"

His cow let out a happy hum as she wriggled against him and Jason played with the moment, tilting his head so he could nibble gently on her petal-shaped ear. He could have spent hour upon hour on her ears, nibbling and kissing them, even running his tongue up and over the soft curve of them. It was such a small part of her body in the grand scheme of things, but it was those little things that made moments they'd want to look back on in the future.

Life… Life was simply made up of moments. And Jason could not help but long for even more of those moments, taking note of the tiny arch in her lower back, how her hips rocked forward just a little more than they had a few seconds before.

"Mmph…" Olivia grumbled good-naturedly against him, half-turning her head so she could look directly at him, though only with one eye. "You know exactly what you're doing to me, don't you? Silly bull…"

He grinned, though there was nothing innocent about the look on his face.

"Oh… I know very well, my dearest."

His words washed over her and Jason pressed on, his paw sliding fully between her thighs, though there was no resistance at all there. She parted her legs willingly for him, water swilling lightly around them, though he had no intent on making things tricky or uncomfortable for the cow in the slightest.

Sex in the bath was overrated, considering how small it was with two bodies in there, though he made a mental note to make sure their next home, when they upgraded, had a bigger bathroom, suitable for a bath they could really enjoy one another in. But he could do other things for Olivia and, honestly, his attention was solely on her as he brushed her pussy with the tips of his fingers, applying no more pressure than strictly necessary in the moment.

"Oh... Jason!"

She wriggled against him, finding it more difficult than ever to stay still. Yet her need mounted as his sheath plumped out against her lower back, her body tucked all the way back between his legs, the bull's knees apart. There was nowhere for the cow to go and Olivia didn't want to be anywhere other than exactly where she was, her lips parted as her tongue flicked out briefly against them and retreated.

"Mm..."

She didn't have to do anything more other than relax into the moment, though Olivia could not help feeling like she should have been doing something more. It was strange for her to so often be in a position where she felt her husband was worshipping her, but, well...he had always been one to put her and her pleasure first and foremost. Yet that did not mean at all that she didn't want to make him feel good too.

There was no space for her, however, to even get her paw around between their bodies, reaching his sheath and growing shaft. However could Jason get hard from just masturbating her? His fingers slid inside, just two, and she rolled her hips forward without actually thinking about what she was doing.

"Oh... Jason... Please..."

"Mmm, no, love," he breathed, kissing and nibbling gently over her neck. "You need to take it easy, you've been doing so much lately. Just let me take care of you."

Heat rose through her, twisting and curling around the core of her being, yet she couldn't do anything about it. With a throaty whine, she shook herself, damp hair clinging to the back of her neck, though Olivia kept it trimmed short, coming down just below her ears. He had a little hair too, though it was darker and mostly resided between his antlers in a cute little tuft.

But her mind slipped away from that notion as he teased the bud of her clit, slipping her folds apart so it peeked out of its hood, though her body was as ready for him as it ever was. He groaned against her back, letting out a low chuff, and she loved knowing she was getting to him too, even though Jason had put her in a position where she wasn't really able to give back all she was receiving.

"Ah… My cow…"

He rumbled throatily, emotion building, though all he had to do was please her. His fingers teased inside her, pumping deep and dragging back out over her clit. Yet that soft button of flesh was where most of her pleasure was concentrated as he wasn't quite able to get his fingers curled up inside her to please the sensitive nerves inside her pussy from that angle.

Jason would find a way, somehow, circling her clit and pulling her flesh gently with the lure of his touch, making sure she was stimulated. He couldn't help his shaft rising, filling out his sheath more than it had already, though it was a moderate length. It fitted his partner perfectly, though and that was all that mattered there, the length very lightly curved with a narrower, tapered tip.

It swelled to full hardness, grinding into her rump, and he let out an apologetic chuff, nostrils twitching. But the moment was not for him, even though he didn't want to be making a point of his need at that time, not as he shifted his weight, the water swilling up against the lip of the bath. They couldn't move too much without making a mess, the bubbles sinking down a little more, though they had only been present for a little tease and flavour in the moment.

How could he put together a romantic bath for her, after all, without the aid of bubbles?

"Mmmmm…"

His cow settled a little more against him, succumbing to pleasure, though her knees tried to come out further against his, pressing into them. He had to hold her there, purely for the lure of her pleasure – and they couldn't exactly just easily get out of the bath, not when needs were rising like that. It was one of the most comfortable positions for Olivia with her belly, and he splayed the fingers of his free paw out over it, admiring the gentle curve and swell of it.

Oh, it would not be long before their little calf was born… And he couldn't wait to welcome them into the world.

Jason would always have time in his life and day, of course, for Olivia, however, despite how things were going to change.

"Mmm, don't think about anything else, darling," he breathed, breath tickling her ear. "You only have to relax, only have to enjoy…"

She wanted to push back against that, to make things more even-handed between them, but, well…he didn't let her. She'd just have to pay him back in sweet pleasure another time as he rubbed her clit, his fingers playing and teasing with her body, even as Olivia's shuddering trembles against him increased in frequency and fervour.

"Mmm… Yes… Oh… Ohhh, that feels…"

"Good, honey?"

He chuckled against her, revelling in her pleasure, though he enjoyed the moments passing through him, trying to commit every second to memory the best he could. Of course, that wasn't possible, but he wanted to languish there, in the heat of the bath, the bubbles catching the candlelight as it glanced off their lightly reflective surfaces. They were like moments too, passing by, and the harder Jason tried to hold on to them, the swifter they popped.

Yet he grounded himself in the sensation of her body against his, hips shifting and trying to push back. He guided her there, her body tingling – he was sure of it – as the lure of orgasm pulled her more and more, closer and closer to the edge. There was only one way for Olivia to go, after all, and he licked his lips, almost as hungry to give her pleasure as his shaft was, clearly, for a bit of pleasure of its own.

The cow shuddered bodily, the biggest ripple yet coursing through her, yet she didn't want to hold back, not as ripples teased deeper and deeper. The tremors pulled at her body, every sensation feeling just a little different in the bath, rather than on the bed. The smooth surface of the bath slipped against her as she pressed into his solid muscle, the scents in the air playing against her nose.

She inhaled deeply, but even that was not enough to let her settle – and climax came with a flaring burst of raw need.

She groaned, twitching and shuddering, her body trying to find a way to release its need in a physical manner, though she had to ease through the moment, to let orgasm come by his paw at its own pace. It was out of her control and there was something delicious about that too for Olivia, as if a deeper part of her soul liked being able to hand that over to her husband.

And he would take it each and every time his wife wanted him to hold it, gently guiding her and taking charge of her pleasure. Her body twitched and rocked against him as she moaned and rode out her climax, deep ripples of pleasure coursing through her body, though Jason held her tightly, his fingers working and pumping inside her, the thumb and heel of his paw ground over her clit just for a little more sensation.

Olivia cried out, moisture in the corners of her eyes, forced to relish in the moment, the rise and fall of pleasure, though it took a while to ebb from her form. Her pussy squeezed around his fingers, glad of something to grip and tease, though it was still not the cock she wanted inside her, her body craving something carnal she could push into.

"Mmmm…"

She hummed faintly, relaxing against him as the waves tapered down, though he was right there to hold her, gently washing her off after her climax.

"Don't worry, darling, I've got you."

A small part of her took over, relaxing into the sensation and feeling of being looked after and cared for so intimately, though she knew Jason would have done it whether she was pregnant. He cleaned her fur with her favourite shower scrub and washed her hair for her, though even the cow had to acknowledge she was taking rather longer than usual to come back to herself again after climax. It seemed to be something that had come throughout her pregnancy, becoming increasingly potent as her body nursed a new life.

But he was there for her and helped her out of the bath too, making sure everything was taken care of, nothing for Olivia to think about. She whimpered softly, turning her head to brush a kiss on to his cheek, though she knew he understood what she was going through. With how randy she'd been throughout her pregnancy, they had certainly had more than enough sex and experience the whole time!

Once they were done drying off in front of the wall-mounted fur-drier (that had been an investment he would never regret, despite the luxury cost), he led her gently to the bedroom, taking his time. Olivia was slower than she usually was with the weight of her pregnant belly guiding her there, though he didn't make a note or a comment on it, merely going along with her.

Besides, he could lay her back on the bed as soon as they were inside the bedroom, her legs spread for him willingly, though the round rise of her belly tended to get in the way. He dropped to his knees before the foot of the bed, kissing his way slowly up her legs, nuzzling up into her inner thighs where her short coat of fur was at its softest and fluffiest.

"Mmm…"

"Ah, honey…" Olivia breathed, squirming in place, though the weight of her belly kept her there, even if she couldn't really tense her abdominal muscles anymore. "You don't have to do that again, it's okay… I want you to have fun too!"

But Jason was having all the fun he wanted in that moment, nuzzling up and over the rounded swell of her stomach, his paw reverently splayed over the top of it. He took a sharp intake of air as a small kick rose against his paw, though that was not the moment for Jason to stay there and savour it, not when his cow was already needy.

She spread her legs a little more for him, but Jason obligingly let her slide her long, fine legs up and over his shoulders, so Olivia didn't have to feel like she was being dragged down off the edge of the bed. It gave her more support and naturally guided his muzzle right down against the soft folds of her pussy, the warm tease of her arousal glistening just barely on her folds. Ah, she was so horny through her pregnancy and he was more than ready to help her out with that, even if she had truly only just got off.

There was plenty of time for both of them that night, if Olivia insisted he took his pleasure too. Truthfully, Jason would have been more than happy to go without it, as long as it meant he could please her and snake his long tongue up inside her pussy, gently parting her folds.

"Oh!"

The cow arched up against his touch – well, the muscles that did that for her tried to tighten – and quivered in place, her lips parted lightly in a long, drawn-out moan. Yet he did not pause, not as his tongue slid deeper, curling up against her G-spot as he tried to source the angle and stroke, that night, which would have her crying out in orgasm all over again. Nothing was ever the same twice in a row, it had to be said, and personal likes were always changing.

He loved that change, the little twists and shifts in their bodies keeping them interested and seeing just where things would go, that time, in the bedroom with one another. There was always room for experimentation as he lapped up slowly and deeply into her, letting his tongue stroke through her pussy, caressing the soft velvet of her passage.

Yet it was her arousal, captured by his tongue, Jason could not help moaning at, the sweet tanginess sinking into his mouth. He swallowed it down as if it was the greatest aphrodisiac in the world and yet took his time about it, licking eagerly, always knowing there was more to come. If he had anything to say about all of it, that was...

He moaned into her sex as his aching member throbbed back to full hardness all over again. He needed her and ached for her – though how was he supposed to adore and worship her and take care of her needs, all at the same time?

It would have to come, one way or the other, for there was balance in everything. Jason grunted as he licked up into her pussy, feeling the clench of her sex around him, muscles twitching and pulling around his tongue. Oh, Olivia was so needy, her body aching for climax, and he longed to give that to her, even as her pants came in shorter and shorter gasps of air.

"Mmm… Oh… Jason… I want to feel you too…"

"Mmmph?"

He didn't raise his head for a moment, too invested in eating her out, the sweet tanginess of her pussy clinging to his tongue. Jason groaned into her sex, eyes barely even open, the petal of her folds spreading against his tongue.

Yet when his cow's paw brushed his head, he perked up again, tail twitching, though her fingers withdrew, stroking one of his antlers.

"Mm?"

He blinked up at her, his shaft throbbing so fervently he could barely catch himself again. It was hard to think when he was as aroused as he was, his balls aching, though he had spent his need with her only the other night.

Olivia simply had that effect on him, time after time again. She coaxed him up and over her, the round of her belly trapped softly between their bodies, and kissed him, his arms framing her head as he took care not to knock her, in the process, with his antlers.

She kissed him deeply, though the wetness between her thighs was not to be ignored either as she huffed hotly into the kiss, lingering there, enjoying the moment. Her tongue teased his and pulled back, brushing her snout tenderly against his.

"Mmm... Please... I want you inside me," she said, leaving no doubt as to what she wanted from him. "Please... Up on the bed, with me?"

He helped her up, not able to resist her charm in the slightest – especially when it came to fulfilling her needs. Yet it was difficult for the cow to get into her preferred position for sex, on all fours, though she would just about get used to how her centre of gravity had changed by the time her pregnancy came to its natural close. His paws guided her, however, drawing her hips back to him as he knelt behind her, settling a pillow under Olivia too, just in case she wanted to slump down on to it and get a little extra support.

If she wanted to be in a different position, at any time, the bull would always make sure to accommodate that for her, attentive to her needs. Yet Jason didn't need to do anything more than slide his shaft into the heat of her sex, her wetness closing around him.

"Oof..."

The bull trembled, the reverberation rolling through his body, thighs tense with need. He didn't want to lose control and thrust wildly, yet the heat of her body called him on a more primal level. Of course, there was no need to worry about a condom when she was already heavily pregnant, though Jason still very much adored the sensation of skin-on-skin contact.

"Mmmm..."

He licked his lips as she rocked back faintly against him, using the leverage she had on the bed to grind back on to his cock. Oh, how he loved that feeling, though it made his head swim pleasantly as she squeezed around him. Olivia just seemed to know exactly what she needed to do to please him, without even trying. Or maybe the cow always was trying, rocking and grinding on to him with soft need, her wetness trickling out around the join of their bodies.

"Mmm… Yes…"

Her breathy moans and pants were all he needed as he ground in, thrusting hard enough for his hips to make a light slap against her backside as he thrust. Yet it was far from the only sound in their bedroom, the rich, purple bedsheets rumpling under them, though they had thrown off the big duvet in favour of something lighter and softer in the warmer months of the year.

The curtains had not been drawn and Jason caught a glimpse of his reflection, paired with his lover, as he thrust deep, using every inch of his cock as his paw crept around under her body. Torn between caressing her pussy and smoothing the flat of his paw over her pregnant belly, the bull had to settle on pleasing her, though he longed to feel more kicks and twitches from within her belly too.

That would come, yes… When they were curled up, sweetly, in bed afterwards, enjoying one another and letting the world pass by without noticing them. That space was theirs and theirs alone as Jason humped and ground, another groan tearing itself from his lips as he thrust harder still.

"Unff… Ah… Olivia…"

She whimpered his name back to him, her torso easing down on to the pillow he had laid there for her, though the bull didn't stop thrusting. Not even with his paw pinned between the pillow and her body, rubbing her clit, even if there wasn't anything soft or refined about what he was doing in that moment. It was difficult to be delicate when she was shuddering against him, his hips briefly flush to her rump before pulling back again.

He had to have it, that lure of orgasm – especially as his sweet cow moaned on his cock, her pussy trembling and clenching around him as another climax dragged her away. And yet she was still right there with him, his breath whipped away by the sheer, raw force of her lust, amazed she could still make him feel like that after so long together.

Yet there was always more to come, step by step and moment by moment. There would always be more to uncover and experience with one another, even if the elk couple was treading over old ground. He grunted as he thrust harder, driven by her moans, her faint whispers begging for him to take her, to spend himself inside her.

"Please… I need… Oh!"

If that was what his sweetheart yearned for, he'd give it to her again and again, absolutely everything and anything she wanted, time after time again. He gasped, letting out a chuff – and didn't hold back for a single moment more as his whole body juddered up to her, sinking deep, releasing his load.

Ropes of hot, creamy cum splattered up inside her, though the cow didn't feel it all intimately, not like that. Swimming in a haze of orgasm, warmth flooding her right down to her fingers and cloven hooves, she gasped breathlessly, raking in much-needed air to her lungs, though there was only so much she could do. Olivia was only there to ride out her own pleasure all over again, the trickle of his seed leaking out around the base of his shaft, where their bodies joined, more alluring to her.

Yet she allowed the warmth of him to melt into her as, slowly, he spent every last drop he had inside her, a bigger orgasm than, honestly, Olivia had expected from him. Yet she remained there, steadying herself, her pussy pulling and rippling around his member, though there was nothing about that she could control. And that was okay too as she rested, her head down, letting him spend himself to completion before he rolled, very gently, to the side, pulling her with him.

"Oof…"

"Sorry, love."

The position, rolling into spooning, tugged at her weight and she rested a paw on her belly, comforting herself, even if it was only a momentary discomfort. It was worth it to relax there, to enjoy the moment, licking her lips and panting faintly even as she came back to her own sense of reality.

Yet it was all right in her little corner of the world, rolling her hips back sensually into him while her life mate caressed her belly, adoring the back of her neck and around the corner of her jaw with tiny, soft kisses. No words needed to be exchanged as he exhaled, chest rising and falling more sharply as he caught his breath, but they nestled into one another's presence, the moment everything it needed to be for them.

"Mmm…"

Everything would change for the better once their calf was born, but, until then, he settled and caressed her stomach, sliding his fingers back and forth, the thick, chunky hoof-like fingertips sliding easily over her flesh. He took his time, rubbing in soft circles, applying only a little pressure.

Just as she liked it.

"Mmm… I love you so much."

"And I love you too, darling," she breathed in turn. "I don't know what I'd do without you in my life."

It was true and it always would be true as they relaxed there, dozing in and out of a light sleep, tails twitching, his head tipped back so his rack of antlers rested on the pillow more comfortably.

Together, they flourished.
But, in herself, his sweet cow simply *glowed*.

# Passion

Shanna smiled, the pale, white unicorn anthro sitting up straight with her partner sitting behind her. The hippogriff's muscular legs were spread so her buttocks teased lightly back against his crotch, but, well: it was not as if they didn't know how their evening was going to go.

Sitting on the bank above the curve of the river, the pair were right where they needed to be, although they were taking a risk being so open about things. Of course, they were both naked, for there were few bounds around nudity in their cultures, the hippogriff living in a small town and the unicorn living close to her herd out in the forest. They both lived quite different lives with Shanna preferring to be closer to nature and living a simple life while the hippogriff worked in technology.

Such was the way of their world that anthros of all kinds could come together, even though it was, quite often, frowned on to grow too close. Rules like that, unspoken, were truly arbitrary.

Which was exactly why Shanna and Glamor had to keep their relationship quieter. They didn't make a big song and dance about meeting up, choosing outdoor pursuits in peaceful areas more often than not – though that suited them both.

Of course, what they had in mind to consummate was risky, so very risky. He was a hippogriff anthro, with an equine lower half and an avian upper body, like that of a sleek, powerful bird of prey. Shanna was a unicorn – and they needed no further explanation as to how well their bodies were designed for one another.

His wings extended from his back, arching out from the points of his shoulder blades where there was additional muscle and sinew there to allow him full control of them. He could fly short distances with his wings, though it was a tricky endeavour for the hippogriff, considering that his body was a little on the heavier side and more densely muscled. He would have had to work out a lot more than he did to be able to take on longer distances in the air, though it was still very much possible.

The wings banded with grey and black, the feathers on his upper half boasting the same shades. His chest was broad, to match his strong, equine lower half, with a darker grey base and white flecked feathers adding definition there. Unlike with some anthros, the feathers and hair on his body were both close enough to his flesh that they showed his muscle easily, not softening or hiding the edges in the slightest.

His horse lower half was that of a dappled grey equine, with a sheath and set of balls to match. Sometimes Glamor worked from home and enjoyed having the ability to free his genitals at that time, though it was still considered polite to be professionally dressed for any meetings he had to attend. Going about in most open spaces, however, was perfectly fine in any state of undress, as long as nothing sexual was going on.

However, when there was no one else around…all bets were off and there was simply no reason for anyone to hold back. It was as private as they could have liked there, their bags set aside with their clothes folded, perhaps creased, smartly away.

He ran his fingers, with bird-like talons, down her arm, smiling with an open beak at how she reacted to even that light touch. Oh, Shanna would always captivate him. But only time would tell just how their relationship would develop, though he had high hopes for staying by her side until the end of his days.

It would be the hippogriff's honour.

His tail flicked as she let out a breathy moan, her horn glowing faintly with her inner essence.

"Ah, Glamor," she groaned, tipping her head back as he ran a claw up her bare neck, teasing her exposed skin but never breaking it. "I don't know how I could ever resist you."

"I was never here to take choice away from you, my sweet," he crooned faintly, though there was still the glimmer of a predatory note in his tone. "Please, never worry yourself about that. This is all your choice. I know what I want, but I never want to pressure you."

She shuddered against him, half-turning her head so she could press her cheek to his chest. The hippogriff was a good foot and a half taller than her, though the unicorn's heart sung for the size difference between them. Her power lay in her magic as she trembled there, though her body was light and lithe, as if she was built for speed and long-distance running. Her coat was a pure white, only tarnished by the faintest of green marks on her hip from where she had lain down in the grass with Glamor, yet her mane and tail stole the show. In a cascade of pink, they drew the eye with their curls and waves, turning heads whenever she was seen.

It was a good thing herbivores were vegetarians, as she would not have made much of a hunter with a mane like that. Her tail was not a fall of simple hair like Glamor's, but draped along a length that was more feline in its appearance, or draconian, for there was a fair deal of flexibility in the full length of it. The pink spill of hair draped down two feet of the length, from the tip, and she flicked it faintly across the grass.

Although Shanna's eyes were on the glittering river as the sun dipped towards the horizon at the tail end of the day, her attention was fully focused on her lover and no one else than that. She couldn't think about anything other than the heat of his body against her and how her own body sang for his.

She wanted him… And the time had come to make the decision as to whether they were going to take their relationship to the next natural phase, or not. There was no pressure, exactly as the hippogriff had said, but Shanna craved it.

"I know this is a risk," she breathed, though her choice had already been made. "We're so similar… I can't have a barrier between us, not with my magic. It will simply melt away if it's made of synthetic material."

"I know, darling," he crooned lightly, preening her mane with his beak, though Glamor was careful not to mess it up too much. "It's okay. As long as you are okay with it, so am I. But it must be our decision, together."

Shanna knew that and she slipped around in the hippogriff's arms to face him, sliding her hands up his bare chest. Some anthros referred to their hands as "paws," but the unicorn mare had a more particular way of thinking about things. Where horses didn't have paws, it didn't make sense to her for unicorns to have to deal with that too.

But the hippogriff was all she wanted and Shanna was already committed to her decision. With her heart surging, she pressed her bare breasts up against his chest and leaned into his hold, as if all she had in mind was to hungrily devour his mouth with hers.

Of course, his avian beak was trickier for her soft lips to mould to than those of another unicorn's would have been. But Shanna wouldn't have it any other way as she turned her head a little, so her lips better fit against his beak.

The hippogriff's tongue was long and sinuous, thinner than hers, though not as flexible as some anthro species, who had ridiculously long appendages tucked within their mouths. His curled and twisted up against her broader, fleshier tongue, though Shanna would not have honestly wanted anything different.

Glamor was the only one she'd ever kissed and the first she was going to make love with too. Such a length of shaft could not be hidden away forever and he grunted into her mouth as his arousal flowed forth. It pushed from his sheath, forcing the tuck of flesh to stretch around it, but neither hippogriff nor unicorn paid it any mind in the moment. They didn't need to, too entranced by each other.

Yet it swelled increasingly, showing off that equine part of him as the wrinkled flesh of Glamor's cock smoothed out, bit by bit. The medial ring popped out, although the head remained softer in a mushroom-like shape, despite being a little flatter than some with equine shafts. Some had engorged flares even before orgasm, yet that was not the case for Glamor.

It would be easier for Shanna to take inside her like that, after all, which was only a benefit to both of them. His cock was a smooth pink all over with a few grey speckles near the base, but they were not all that obvious. She ground against him lightly, trapping his cock between their stomachs, yet Shanna didn't grasp it, not yet.

There was more than enough time for them to savour the moment, even if breeding was in order. They didn't know whether their tryst would result in a foal, of course, but it was very likely if he pressed into her soft folds with nothing around his cock. As they'd discussed, unicorn magic meant that synthetic materials simply didn't work when it came to protection.

So, they had to take the risk and they had to be committed to each other above all else. Glamor's head swam pleasantly and his wings flapped, extending out from his shoulder blades as if his body was struggling to keep up with everything the unicorn mare was throwing at him. Never before had such lust swelled within him, the aching throb of his cock making even Glamor tremble. The hippogriff tried to control himself but not even he could resist a subtle roll of his hips as his cock throbbed, his abdominal muscles clenching to make his shaft jostle and bump. It was a manner of equine masturbation that was more useful to those who didn't have hands, but Glamor appreciated and experimented with it sometimes.

It would not be needed with his unicorn, however, as they broke the kiss. A light string of saliva connected her lips to his beak for a fraction of a moment before breaking: the bond between them would never be broken. For there was far more between them than the lure of sexual fervour, but deeply rooted passion woven through their bodies.

One would not be able to exist without the other after that evening together, the sun setting to paint ruby shades across the glittering river. Yet neither noticed, too wrapped up in each other, as her hand trailed a little shyly down his chest to his abdomen, and lower still.

"May I?" She breathed, as if she feared being turned down. "I don't know how to do this."

Glamor chuffed, feathers fluffing up lightly as his equine tail swished.

"That's okay, I'll be here for you," he murmured soothingly, taking her hand and clasping it to his chest, letting her feel the pounding beat of his heart. "And I don't exactly have all that much experience too, my dear Shanna. We are in this together."

Where Shanna was a virgin, Glamor was not. That didn't matter as he grunted and laid back under her pressure, her hand in the middle of his chest as he tried to lie down as gently as he was able. His wings fanned out to either side of his body as he lay back, making sure not to crush them. As strong as they were, there were many sensitive bones in there that could be easily broken too.

The hippogriff's tail tried to lift as Shanna kissed her way down his body, not that the mare had not explored him like that before. It was a new manner of exploration, however, and one that the hippogriff invited gladly as his dock twitched. The velvety flesh at the base of his tail, where the hairs spilled from, was longer and thicker than many considered, but Shanna would learn just how sensitive it was with the hippogriff in due course.

The unicorn shook faintly as she reached for his cock, though she'd seen it before. She just had not touched and held him intimately with the intent of going all the way before at any time prior. Shanna moaned faintly, yet the unicorn's breath ghosted across the head of his cock as she gently clasped it in her hand.

Her fingers would not fold all the way around his member and she grunted faintly, marvelling at how thick around it was. However it would all fit inside her was beyond her imagination, though she was sure it would not be a problem at all. It was the kind of cock, after all, that her body was made for, so she would stretch. With magic running through her veins, things would be even easier, despite his size.

Yet the stretch would be immense, Shanna thought with a lustful little quiver, as he drove into her. She could almost imagine it right there and then, although she had no prior experience to go off, aside from how his fingers and tongue had felt inside her before. Her mind clung to the notion of her pussy stretching, wider and wider, clinging to his shaft as the hippogriff eased inside in that sweet, first penetration.

"I want to explore every inch of you," she hissed out through her teeth, the long lash of her tail sweeping excitedly. "Everything… Oh, Glamor…"

"Mmm, it's okay, darling, it's okay," he said, soothing her excitement by cupping her cheek with his fingers and talons. "Take your time. I have all the time in the world for you."

"Mm, I know, sweetheart. And I the same for you, always and forever."

She winked up at him, on all fours, her buttocks swaying lightly from side to side, though it was a very subtle shift in her body. Brushing her lips over his cock, she investigated his length as if it really was the first time she'd ever seen it, though it was the mare's excitement, in the end, that would get the best of her.

Her pussy winked and pulled as if trying to invite him into her, even if her back end was pointed away from the hippogriff. She was too caught up in the moment and his throbbing hard-on, visible pulses running through his member, to care about it. Yet that insidious, trickling heat still warmed her through as the mare panted lightly, her breath tickling his cock while she let her lips fold sensually around the head.

The effect on Glamor was electric, the hippogriff kicking out and letting out a sound between a screech and a neigh, both together. Yet she kept pushing down, testing how far her jaw could stretch to take his cock into her mouth. Her longer muzzle was a better shape for taking his length than that of many others, though there was an awful lot of his cock to take in.

She would do her best, knowing there was no right or wrong answer to how they chose to enjoy one another. Suckling around his cock lightly, she pulled her lips up to his light flare, which fleshed out just a little more within her mouth. Her tongue swept around the underside of the glands before playing across the spongy tip, curiously investigating the slit in the head. He nickered and grunted, wings fluttering, and Shanna had to resist the urge to push on his sensitivity and see just how far she could take it.

The hippogriff held back as much as he could, though he couldn't resist winding and running his fingers through her mane, over and over again. Her ears were so cute and yet her mouth hid something sultry indeed, that fleshy length of her tongue cupping the underside and sweeping back up towards the head again. Glamor guided her very gently as she bobbed her head on his shaft, pressing the tip into the back of her throat as she sank past the medial ring and tested out just where her own limits lay.

The unicorn was beautiful exactly as she was, however, and he panted her name as she gave him the most mind-blowing blowjob of his life. Of course, it was her first, but it was who Glamor was with that made it as special as it was for him. She drooled a little around his cock as she sucked on him, a light sheen of saliva coating his exposed length whenever it was revealed.

The unicorn lost herself in her own world, yet she couldn't deny her need. It was there as the presence of a hard and ready male set off her blood singing, aching with a whisper of power. Shanna didn't use her powers all that often, not for what the other unicorns did, but she would find her calling and place in time. Before then, all she needed to focus on in the moment was Glamor.

"Mmm, my sweet, you don't have to give all your attention to me."

Glamor drew her up and off his cock, though she whimpered and tried to keep his shaft inside her lips for as long as possible. Yet the hippogriff wanted to show her more pleasure still, sitting up again as he drew her over his legs and into his lap. Her knees went to either side of his body instinctively, though Glamor wasn't intended for his cock to spring up against her butt as insistently as it did.

Shanna groaned, yet the unicorn unravelled before her lover as the hippogriff palmed her pussy, sliding two fingers back and forth through her wet folds. He had to be careful of his talons, of course, but Glamor had already filed down a couple to make sure they wouldn't run any risk of hurting her. Grinding them slowly up inside her pussy, he penetrated her patiently; even the hippogriff let out a light gasp at how wet she was.

Shanna was practically soaked as she worked his fingers back and forth inside her, letting her whine and hump on to his hand. She was usually so put together and composed that it was truly a thing of beauty to see her come undone before him, as if the hippogriff was the only one she ever could have trusted with such an intimate part of her. She was far from frail, though someone had to be vulnerable to open up in such a manner, his fingers curling up inside her pussy.

"Oh!"

The sharp cry left her suddenly as if even the unicorn was surprised to feel her lips let such a sound out. Shanna ground against his fingers with increasing need and it was in that moment Glamor knew their first time together would not last quite as long as the gryphon anticipated.

That was okay, however; that was what second and third rounds were for. Anything his unicorn desired she could have. As she panted heavily, lips agape and nostrils flaring with every drag of breath, he let her rise a little higher, supporting her hips. His fingers pulled from her pussy, slurping forth with a drooling dose of her arousal. There was no question at all regarding her readiness.

Shanna scrambled to get into position, her body seeming to jerk forward against Glamor, knowing what it needed even before the notion had fully formed in her mind. She nickered throatily, eyes half-lidded with desire, and kissed the edge of his beak as he nudged his cock under her, between her legs. The thick tip pushed against her folds, which were still pulled apart a little from the passage of his fingers. Her head spun pleasantly, a little dizzy – and yet rooted in place all the same.

It didn't have to make sense with her, not as she met Glamor's gaze and nodded.

"I want you," she said, confirming what they already knew. "I will always want you, Glamor. Let me be yours, and you be mine."

The hippogriff grunted and kissed her passionately, letting her hips sink towards him. It was all up to her how swiftly she took his shaft bare for the first time, though he held his cock in position for her. At first it seemed like her pussy wasn't going to allow his cock into her body, his length bowing slightly, but it was not to be. For his shaft popped inside her as she gasped into his mouth, eyelashes fluttering. They were too close and wanton to desire breaking the kiss, his tongue curving up inside her mouth as he explored her in a way he never had before.

Glamor's feathers puffed up as he throbbed inside the mare, the beauty of his life. She was so much more than simply gorgeous, however, with her sharp wits and bright mind. Only in time would he come to learn every nuance of her, every little secret she'd never shared with anyone else at all.

"Ohh…"

He let a soft moan out into her lips as she sank lower, her legs trembling. She'd had to come up on to her cloven hooves at first, to get to the right height for his cock, though it looked like Shanna was more than ready to drop back to her knees as she sank lower and lower. With the medial ring teasing up against her pussy, the mare quivered against him, lips shifting against his beak.

Shanna gasped and let the hippogriff take over, for she didn't quite know what to do. Her pussy burned pleasantly without a drop of pain as if his shaft was reaching, already, into the very core of her being. How could he possibly be that deep inside her? The unicorn hardly even cared as her pussy flexed and pulled around him as if her body was trying to draw his shaft deeper still, but it was not under her control.

Not anymore, not as he guided her and helped her ride that portion of his cock that she'd already taken. Slowly, he helped her ease down a little further, grinding the head of his cock deeper into the clasping wetness of her folds, but he did not yet bottom out inside her. Her passage accommodated every inch of him that it could as the medial ring disappeared and she leaned heavily against his chest.

"Mm, take it easy, my darling…"

He breathed her name, but Shanna was already gone, whinnying shrilly as her tail curled around his calf and orgasm hit her. With a rush of her juices, she sank lower still, the additional lubrication helping her clenching, pulling sex to take even more of him. It was right at the moment it mattered, drawing his need right along with hers, his cock flexing and throbbing as if he was going to lose control.

They'd already discussed him cumming inside her so that was not something Glamor had to pause to consider. His heart surged and he parted his beak in a gryphon smile, nibbling softly on her neck while she came back to herself, impaled on his cock. Yet his sweet mare held tightly on to his shoulders as she rocked and ground her hips, rising and falling as if struck by a need she had not even known existed.

Shanna would be a sexual force to be reckoned with, all in time. But he speared into her with a roll of his hips, legs bending so he had a little more leverage.

She moaned, letting him nip at her bare neck as she rocked up and down on his cock, a little more of his shaft disappearing into her every time. The unicorn trembled before him and Glamor got to feel every moment, from the clench of her pussy to how her breasts gently brushed his chest. There were so many sensations all coming up against one another that it was impossible even for the hippogriff to cling on to each and every last one.

So, he would have to be with Shanna repeatedly so he could enjoy every little moment as if it was his last, lips parted and need swelling through him. His cock throbbed and, dimly, the hippogriff was aware of the head of his cock flaring out, dragging more tenaciously against her velvety passage. The unicorn bucked instinctively against him, pulled by the draw of it, and he tried to capture her lips once again with his beak.

It was not to be so, however, not as his balls ached and throbbed. Desire rolled within him and something deeper still lurched, but he couldn't hold back. It simply was not for the gryphon, not in the slightest, not as he huffed and panted heavily through his nares, the unicorn keening out on his shaft all over again.

Shanna lost herself in another rush of her arousal, pussy twitching around him as it rhythmically rippled. Yet her attention was on her partner even as her body warmed through with a glow, spreading to even her extremities.

The unicorn was too busy watching the conflicting emotions on her partner's face, however, the slight narrowing of his eyes that meant he was having trouble. Yet as nearly the full length of his cock buried itself inside her, her pussy stretched into a tight, lewd hug around his shaft, she caught the throb of need.

Not hers but his. Shanna clung to him as he rocked forward against her suddenly, spearing into her pussy as she gripped it too tightly. Yet it was not enough to stop him grinding into her pussy as deep as it was possible to go, dragging at breath that didn't quite want to come to her lungs.

The hippogriff shrieked like a beast of the wilds as orgasm swelled through him, nuts churning as he spent long, sticky ropes of seed up into her. Every pulse rolled down his cock noticeably, straining her pussy ever so slightly more, the head flared to its greatest extent. Yet he could not halt their liaison as he helped her ride him, the buck and grind of her hips purely hypnotic.

He spent himself inside her, bareback, and the moment was so much more than that. They knew all that would come of their liaison, the unfertilised eggs inside her that his sperm was rushing towards even at that moment. In the months to come, her belly would swell with evidence of their tryst and everyone could come to know the two of them were together.

They never had any need to hide their love for one another but raising a little foal together would be the next great adventure for them. As his cock stayed hard inside her, Shanna picked up her head with a little gleam in her eye.

"How would you like to make quite sure," she said breathily, "that there really is a foal growing soon in my womb?"

He grinned, clicking the edges of his beak together.

"Oh, I want nothing more, darling. Always and forever, I am yours."

Together, they rocked back and forth, letting lust guide them as to where to go next. There was nothing to hold them back, even as twilight fell around them, fireflies lifting from the grass.

In passion, they found one another. And they'd never again leave.

Thank you for reading and I hope that everything was very much enjoyed!


Ready for more? Check out my author website for more furry fiction and where you can purchase my books!


https://linktr.ee/amethystmare


Cover art illustrated by verysweetpotato; they are contactable via Twitter for work enquiries.

twitter.com/AlexandrCorvin